Millie's Courageous Days

BOOK TWO
of the
A Life of Faith:
Millie Keith
Series

Based on the beloved books by
Martha Finley

MCP
Mission City Press
Franklin, Tennessee

Book Two of the *A Life of Faith: Millie Keith* Series

Millie's Courageous Days
Copyright © 2001, Mission City Press, Inc. All Rights Reserved.

Published by Mission City Press, Inc.

This book is based on the *Mildred Keith* novels written by Martha Finley and first published in 1876 by Dodd, Mead & Company.

Adaptation Written by:	Kersten Hamilton
Cover & Interior Design:	Richmond & Williams
Cover Photography:	Michelle Grisco Photography
Typesetting:	BookSetters

Unless otherwise indicated, all Scripture references are from the Holy Bible, New International Version (NIV). Copyright © 1973, 1978, 1984 by International Bible Society. Used by permission of Zondervan Publishing House, Grand Rapids, MI. All rights reserved.

Millie Keith and *A Life of Faith* are trademarks of Mission City Press, Inc.

For more information, write to Mission City Press at P.O. Box 681913, Franklin, Tennessee 37068-1913, or visit our Web Site at:

www.alifeoffaith.com

Library of Congress Catalog Card Number: 2001118430
Finley, Martha
      Millie's Courageous Days
      Book Two of the *A Life of Faith: Millie Keith* Series
      ISBN: 1-928749-10-0

Printed in the United States of America
1 2 3 4 5 6 7 8 — 06 05 04 03 02 01

DEDICATION

This book is
dedicated to
the memory of
MARTHA FINLEY
1828—1909

*Martha Finley was a woman of God
clearly committed to advancing the cause of Christ
through stories of people who sought
to reflect Christian character in everyday life.
Although written in an era very different from ours,
her works still inspire both young and old
to seek to know and follow the living God.*

*I*n this book, the second of the *A Life of Faith: Millie Keith* Series, you are invited to step once again into our nation's past and follow the adventures of Millie Keith and her large and lively family. Our story resumes in 1833, just before Christmas, in the frontier town of Pleasant Plains, Indiana, which is the new home of the Keith family. The Keiths are determined to live for Christ and be an example of God's love to friends and neighbors. At nearly thirteen, Millie is a strong and growing Christian. But she is about to face life, death, and the greatest challenge her faith has ever had to endure. Through the tragedies and triumphs of their first year in Pleasant Plains, Millie will learn what it means to put her trust in the Lord.

The stories of Mildred Keith by Martha Finley were originally published in 1876, eight years after release of Miss Finley's Elsie Dinsmore series. This book is a careful adaptation of the original Mildred Keith story. In rewriting her story for modern readers, the author has updated the language, strengthened the Christian message, enhanced the plot, and added a number of new features, such as the helpful historical section which follows. Although Millie's life is set in the past, modern girls can now enjoy and relate to her story. Mission City Press is pleased to bring Millie Keith back to life for today's generation of readers.

∾ Life and Health in Millie's World ∾

The 1830s was a fascinating period in American history. The country was exploding westward, becoming established as a world power, defining its identity as a nation, and

exploring the meaning of the Constitution. A girl living in the 1830s could very well have known people who fought for freedom during the Revolutionary War. Two generations had passed while people had been occupied with building a nation, but still a question of freedom remained and a great gulf separated the people of the growing United States of America. Although the Declaration of Independence had stated, "all men are created equal," slavery was an issue over which people in the 1830s were divided.

Abolitionism:

By the middle of the eighteenth century, slavery existed in all thirteen colonies, but it was most important to the economy of the South, where cheap labor was needed for growing cotton. Between 1776 and 1804 all of the northern states abolished slavery. By 1786, organizations had been founded to challenge the existence of slavery in the United States. Groups such as the Pennsylvania Abolition Society, whose membership roles included George Washington, Benjamin Franklin, Thomas Paine, and the Marquis de Lafayette, assisted fugitive slaves in their attempts to flee the South.

In the 1820s, as the second Great Awakening swept through America, men of God such as Lyman Beecher, Nathaniel Taylor, and Charles B. Finney preached that each person had a responsibility to uphold God's will in society. The abolitionist movement of the 1830s sprang from these spiritual roots.

The arguments were fierce and heated. Abolitionists argued that slavery was sinful, and should be abolished everywhere and never allowed in the new territories. Many northerners believed that slavery was not sinful, but it was backward, inefficient, and socially degrading. Southerners

argued that the Bible itself sanctioned slavery, that blacks were unfit for freedom, and that the nation's economy depended on slavery.

In the 1830s, the abolitionist movement united its crusade for the emancipation of all slaves and the end of segregation. In 1830, a man by the name of William Lloyd Garrison began publishing the *Liberator* in Boston. The *Liberator*, which became the most famous abolitionist newspaper, was supported predominantly by free blacks. In fact, many Abolitionists and supporters were free blacks from black churches, organizations, and schools. In 1833, Garrison and sixty other delegates of both races and genders met in Philadelphia (where the Declaration of Independence was signed) to form the American Anti-Slavery Society, which denounced slavery as a sin, endorsed non-violence, and condemned racial prejudice. Hundreds of branches of the Anti-Slavery Society were established throughout the free states. The Abolitionists flooded the North with anti-slavery literature, speakers went to churches and rented halls to denounce slavery, and petitions were circulated demanding that Congress end federal support for slavery.

Their opponents were not silent, however, and seldom polite. Violent mobs attacked abolitionist meetings; mail bags containing abolitionist literature were seized and burned; houses were attacked and destroyed; and Abolitionists beaten. The conscience of a nation was being awakened, and it took great faith and courage to take a stand.

Medicine:

In 1800, most physicians practiced without a degree from a medical college. The trade of medicine was learned

by being an apprentice to a doctor for two to six years. Doctors often did their patients more harm than good. Medicine was advancing, but it still had a long way to go. In the 1830s, medical sciences such as Phrenology, which held that a person's intelligence and even personality were determined by the shape of their skull and the bumps on their head, were considered not only scientific, but also accurate and dependable. Sickness was widely understood to be caused by poisons in the body, and physicians used several means to remove the poison: bloodletting—draining small amounts of blood, either by making a small cut or by applying live leaches to the patient's body; purging—clearing the bowels by means of various purgative medicines; and induced vomiting—used to clear the "poisons" causing stomach pain or general illness.

In the 1830s, anesthetics were unknown. Patients sang hymns, bit down on a soft lead bullet, or used drugs such as alcohol or opium to make the pain of surgery more bearable. Physicians were ignorant of the importance of cleanliness, and many patients who survived operations died from infections caused by dirty operating tools or dressings. A doctor would operate in his street clothes, wearing an apron—often coated with the blood of previous patients.

A typical doctor's bag would contain splints for broken bones; pliers or forceps for removing infected teeth; larger, curved forceps for delivering babies; a stethoscope (which at that time was a wooden tube); and "medicines" such as heroin, which was used as a cough medicine, opium, which was used as a pain remedy, and various "patent" medicines and folk remedies.

The stethoscope, which was invented in 1819, was especially useful to doctors who often had difficulty determining

whether or not a patient was dead. People in a deep coma, or those who were unconscious, gave the appearance of being dead. Occasionally, these dearly departed would suddenly revive at the funeral, to the shock of friends and family. This led to a widespread fear of being buried alive. Crowbars and shovels were sometimes placed in the coffin with a body, just in case the unlucky occupant needed to dig himself or herself out. Wealthy families took the precaution of adding air tubes that led from the coffin to the surface, and leaving servants at the graves to listen for cries for help. The term "dead ringer" comes from the practice of leaving a bell on the grave, attached to a string in the coffin. If you woke suddenly from the dead, you could pull the string, ring the bell, and summon help.

Still, doctors were, for the most part, men of science dedicated to helping others. They spent long hours in their efforts and closely followed the scientific advances of the day, adding knowledge to the profession by their successes and failures.

Letters and diaries of pioneer women from Indiana in the 1830s are like catalogs of symptoms, illness, and complaints. Those who didn't have access to doctors, or who did not trust them, often relied on folk remedies, such as hanging a bag of live insects around the victim's neck to cure whooping cough, or feeding pumpkin seed tea to those with convulsions. Many of the folk remedies were useless, but some had real value.

One of the first physicians we know about was Hippocrates, who lived in the fifth century B.C. He wrote about a bitter powder extracted from willow bark that could ease aches and pains and reduce fevers. In the 1700s, Reverend Edmund Stone described the success of willow bark in the cure of agues.

Foreword

In 1829, a pharmacist named Leroux showed that the active ingredient in willow bark is salicin. Unfortunately, salicin was very hard on the human digestive track, and, in high doses, could even cause bleeding from the stomach. In 1888, a German chemist named Felix Hoffman, working for a chemical company known as Friedrich Bayer & Co., refined the drug, making it easier on the stomach. In 1899 it was given the name we would all become familiar with: aspirin.

The Ague:

"Ague" was a term for fever. There were several kinds of ague, one of the most severe being malaria. Malaria was carried to the frontier in the blood of infected settlers, and transmitted from human to human by the mosquitoes that lived in the swamps. The disease was serious, and could be fatal. Records show that some Indian villages lost nine of every ten people to the disease when it first appeared. The white population, which had access to quinine, had a better survival rate. In 1821, one-eighth of the population of Indianapolis died of fevers.

In the 1830s, the disease was thought to be caused by swamp or night air, hence the name malaria, from the Italian word "mal'aria" meaning bad air. It was also called "marsh miasma." According to George Simpson, Hudson's Bay Company Governor, 1832, "The disease is supposed to be occasioned by the putrid exhalations and penetrating damps which issue from the stagnant water left in the neighboring swamps when the river overflows its banks at the end of the season." The ague was seasonal, occurring from June to October, and could be quite deadly. Once you had malaria, you would be revisited by the symptoms —

chills, fever, and shaking—for the rest of your life. It was so common along the great swamps that people who did not die of it soon accepted the sickness as part of their lives, learning to work even though they felt weak, shaky, and sick. Ague continued to be a life-threatening problem until the swamps were drained.

Women's Work:

In today's society we can hardly conceive of the need for servants, partly because technology has taken over a great deal of our workload. But for women and girls in the 1830s, there was more work to be done than time to do it. There were no washing machines, dishwashers, supermarkets, prepared foods, or pre-made clothing. Thirty percent of a woman's time would be consumed with laundry alone, and then there was cooking, cleaning, and sewing garments for each member of a growing family, and making candles and soap. If the family was wealthy, servants were hired or slaves bought to do the more menial tasks, and the housewife became a manager, overseeing cooks, gardeners, a governess, maids, and stable hands. If the family was not wealthy, the wife and children did the work themselves, often starting before dawn and working late into the night. This left little time for education or bettering one's self.

A girl living in the 1830s would be fascinated by innovations such as friction matches, which had to be struck on sandpaper to ignite them. Food canning was a new and important skill for the housewife, and in 1834 refrigeration was invented. Prior to this, food could only be kept cool in root cellars or wells. Ice boxes, in which blocks of ice were placed to keep food cold, were used in the East, but ice was not available in Pleasant Plains in the summer of 1834. Meat

had to be purchased on daily trips to the butcher shop, or preserved by smoking it or salting it heavily. Fresh meat was a treat. The chain stitch sewing machine had been invented in 1830, but most women still did all of their needlework by hand. Today's modern technology—washing machines, microwaves, dishwashers, and sewing machines—has taken away so much burden from our lives. Millie Keith and her family did not have these advantages, so it took a great deal of hard work and courage to forge a life on the frontier.

KEITH FAMILY TREE

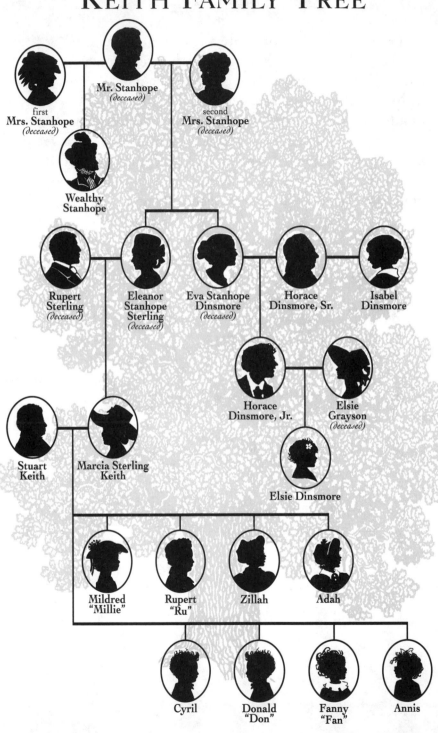

SETTING

*O*ur story begins in winter of 1833 in Pleasant Plains, Indiana, a growing frontier town and the new home of the Keith family.

CHARACTERS

∞ THE KEITH HOUSEHOLD ∞

Stuart Keith — the father of the Keith family; a respected attorney-at-law.

Marcia Keith — the mother of the Keith family and the step-niece of Aunt Wealthy Stanhope.

The Keith children:

> **Mildred Eleanor ("Millie")** — age 13
> **Rupert ("Ru")** — age 12
> **Zillah** — age 10
> **Adah** — age 9
> **Cyril and Donald ("Don")** — age 8, twin boys
> **Fanny ("Fan")** — age 6
> **Annis** — age 2

Wealthy Stanhope — a woman in her mid-50s; Marcia's step-aunt who raised her from infancy; step-aunt to Horace Dinsmore, Jr.

∞ FRIENDS IN PLEASANT PLAINS, INDIANA ∞

Mrs. Prior — the landlady of the Union Hotel.

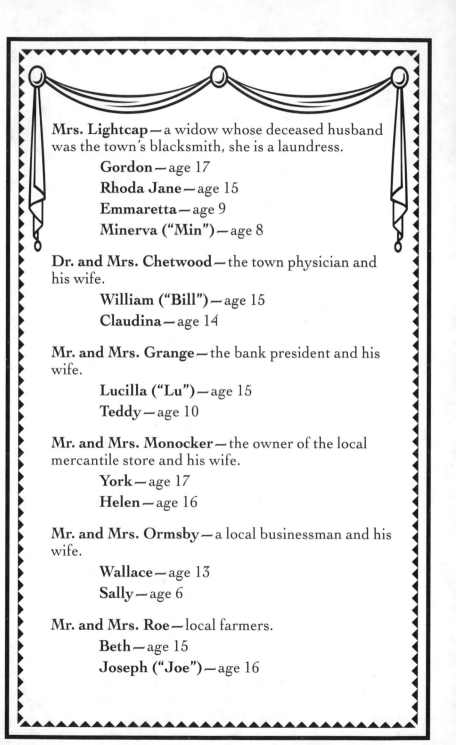

Mrs. Lightcap — a widow whose deceased husband was the town's blacksmith, she is a laundress.

        Gordon — age 17

        Rhoda Jane — age 15

        Emmaretta — age 9

        Minerva ("Min") — age 8

Dr. and Mrs. Chetwood — the town physician and his wife.

        William ("Bill") — age 15

        Claudina — age 14

Mr. and Mrs. Grange — the bank president and his wife.

        Lucilla ("Lu") — age 15

        Teddy — age 10

Mr. and Mrs. Monocker — the owner of the local mercantile store and his wife.

        York — age 17

        Helen — age 16

Mr. and Mrs. Ormsby — a local businessman and his wife.

        Wallace — age 13

        Sally — age 6

Mr. and Mrs. Roe — local farmers.

        Beth — age 15

        Joseph ("Joe") — age 16

Celestia Ann Huntsinger — live-in housekeeper to the Keith family, age 18.

Reverend Matthew Lord — a local minister.

Damaris Drybread — a local teacher, age 23.

Mrs. Prescott — a widowed neighbor.
> **Effie** — age 8

Nicholas Ransquate — a local young man, age 26.

Mr. Tittlebaum — an elderly member of Reverend Lord's church.

∝ OTHERS ∝

Horace Dinsmore, Jr. — Marcia Keith's cousin and the step-nephew of Aunt Wealthy, age 20.

John — Horace Dinsmore, Jr.'s personal valet; a slave from Roselands, the Dinsmore's plantation in the South, age 20.

CHAPTER 1

A Test of Faith

*When I was in distress, I sought
the Lord; at night I stretched
out untiring hands and my
soul refused to be
comforted.*

PSALM 77:2

A Test of Faith

*A*s Millie, Rupert, and Celestia Ann approached the front door of the Big Yellow House, Millie's heart was full of joy. *What a grand time we had tonight!* she thought. *Rhoda Jane was truly the most beautiful girl at the Social, and the green dress fit as if it had been made just for her. It was so exciting to show her God's love! Thank You, Lord, for letting me be part of Your plan. I can't wait to see what You do next!*

Millie turned the doorknob and stepped inside. "Mamma!" she called. "Mamma, we're home!" She pulled off her hat and tossed her muff on the table before she realized that something was very, very wrong. Marcia Keith, Millie's mother, stood beside the couch, one hand over her mouth. Stuart Keith, her father, was kneeling beside it, with a little golden head cradled in his arms. Fanny's face was pale, almost blue in the lamplight, and her eyes were closed.

"Oh, Lord, help us," Aunt Wealthy cried. "I only turned my back for an instant! I went to get Annis some milk . . ." Her voice trickled away into nothing, and then she sobbed.

"What happened?" Rupert asked, pushing past Millie. Nobody answered him, as all were too intent on the still form on the couch.

"She's breathing," Stuart said, stroking Fan's forehead. "She's still breathing. I must go for Dr. Chetwood, Marcia."

Marcia took his place, gently cradling Fan's head. Stuart didn't even look at Rupert and Millie as he went past them into the cold night.

"He forgot his coat," Celestia Ann said.

"What happened?" Millie asked, dropping to her knees beside the couch. "What's wrong with Fan?" She could see a bruise starting to spread like a shadow over the little girl's forehead.

"She fell," Aunt Wealthy said. "Just moments ago. She fell through the door into heaven. Didn't you hear the cry?"

The door into heaven. That's what they called the door from Aunt Wealthy's room that led into thin air above the street. *Pappa nailed it shut when we first moved into the Big Yellow House. How could Fan have fallen through it?* Millie wondered. "Mamma, is she going to be all right?" she asked, taking her little sister's limp hand. "She *is* going to be all right, isn't she?"

Marcia didn't answer. She just kept petting Fan's forehead and whispering to her.

Silent tears were running down Aunt Wealthy's face. Wannago, her little terrier, looked up into her face and whined, then dropped to his belly and crawled to the couch. His little pink tongue darted out, kissing Fan's motionless fingers.

"What can we do?" Rupert asked. "How can we help?"

"Pray," Aunt Wealthy said. "Just pray."

Millie lay her head against the couch. *Don't let Fan die, Lord. Please, let her stay with us.*

No one spoke, and the loud tick-tock of the grandfather clock filled the room. How long would it take Stuart to find the doctor? Dr. Chetwood had been at the Christmas Social, and Stuart might try to find him there first, before going to the Chetwood's home on the other side of town. Stuart was on foot, but Dr. Chetwood had a carriage. Surely they would be here soon. The hands of the clock had never moved so slowly, creeping up to midnight and then down again.

A Test of Faith

Millie couldn't shake the feeling of wrongness in everything—Fan's stillness, the walls between rooms made of curtains, the tables and chairs made of packing crates. What were the Keiths of Lansdale, Ohio, doing in this place? How could they be living in a warehouse with a door that opened into thin air? Millie knew how she would have answered those questions just a few hours before: *It's all God's will. He has a special plan for us!* But now . . . .

At last, they heard the beat of a horse's hooves and the crunch of buggy wheels on the crusted snow. The door burst open and Stuart, Dr. Chetwood, and Reverend Lord, still bundled up from the evening's sleigh ride, appeared. The doctor's professional air had an immediate calming effect. His long black coat, Hessian boots, and even his gold-headed cane gave him an air of efficiency.

Reverend Lord stood behind him, a bit like a nervous scarecrow, in too-short jacket sleeves that allowed his bony wrists to show. Both men required only a moment to take in the situation, and both started for Fan, almost bumping into each other, but Reverend Lord bowed, deferring to the older man.

Dr. Chetwood went straight to the patient, his eyes never leaving her face as he stripped off his soft leather gloves. He warmed his hand for a moment, then felt gently along Fan's neck, turning her head from side to side. He called for a candle, and while Stuart held the flame close to Fan's face, the doctor lifted her eyelids and checked her pupils.

Finally, he stood up. "I'm sorry, Stuart," he said, shaking his head. "She's suffered an injury of the brain. There is nothing we can do but make her comfortable until . . ."

Marcia gasped and ice shot through Millie's heart. Fan was *dying*.

"No!" Aunt Wealthy said. "That is not all we can do! We can plead with the One who holds life and death in His hands!" She sank to her knees and took Fan's little hand in both of hers.

"Dear lady," the doctor said gently, "we can all pray for peace as she slips away . . ."

"No!" Reverend Lord's voice was an echo of Aunt Wealthy's, as if her voice had traveled some distance, found a solid rock wall, and jumped back stronger than before. He stepped out of the shadows and laid his hands on her shoulders.

"Forgive me, Doctor, but that is *not* all we can pray for. God sent me to Pleasant Plains to build a church, and I won't see one of my lambs taken like this!"

"Have you ever seen an injury of this sort, young man?" Dr. Chetwood asked. "I have seen a few. And forgive me," he continued, glancing at Stuart and Marcia, "but I think false hope is cruel. I have never seen a patient recover from an injury like this."

"I never stood in the empty tomb," Reverend Lord countered. "I never put my hands in the Lord's pierced hands and side. But I believe, Doctor. I believe He rose again!"

"This is 1833, Reverend Lord," Dr. Chetwood said, shaking his gray head. "Faith of that kind was necessary in previous centuries before we had physical facts, logic, and science. We are now living in the age of reason, and we must face facts . . ."

"You forget that God is the Creator of science, Doctor," Reverend Lord said gently. "Until He tells me differently, until He takes this sweet child to Himself and I have personally seen His answer, I know where I will be." He sank to his knees beside the couch and pulled a small Bible from

his pocket. "He who dwells in the shelter of the Most High will rest in the shadow of the Almighty," he read. Millie recognized the familiar words of Psalm 91. "I will say of the Lord, 'He is my refuge and my fortress, my God, in whom I trust.' Surely he will save you from the fowler's snare and from deadly pestilence . . ."

Marcia was on her knees beside him now, and Celestia Ann knelt too, her red hair glowing like an ember in Reverend Lord's shadow.

Aunt Wealthy joined in, speaking the psalm by heart: "He will cover you with his feathers, and under his wings you will find refuge; his faithfulness will be your shield and rampart. You will not fear the terror of night, nor the arrow that flies by day, nor the pestilence that stalks in the darkness, nor the plague that destroys at midday. A thousand may fall at your side, ten thousand at your right hand, but it will not come near you . . ."

Dr. Chetwood shook his head and took a small brown bottle from his bag. "It's laudanum," he said. "For Marcia. She may need it when . . ." The doctor paused, then sighed and said, "Send for me if there is any change."

Stuart showed him to the door and shook the doctor's hand without saying a word. Then Stuart came back inside and said, "Let's move her to her own bed."

"No!" said Marcia. "Not upstairs! I . . . I don't want her up there."

"She'll have my bed then," Celestia Ann said.

Stuart carried Fan to the curtained-off corner of the kitchen that was Celestia Ann's room and tucked her into the small, white bed. Millie lit the oil lamp, lowering the wick so there was just enough light in the room to see. Reverend Lord resumed his vigil on his knees, his Bible in

his hand. His voice never faltered as he read psalm after psalm, the words filling the room like a pool of faith.

Millie wanted to kneel and pray with the others, but her body just kept moving — finding pillows, bringing another quilt for Fan, dragging in a rocking chair for her mother and setting it beside the bed, tucking a comforter over her knees.

"Thank you, Millie," Marcia said, looking up. There were no more tears in Marcia's eyes. "Will you care for the other children? I don't think I am up to it right now."

"Yes, Mamma."

Millie climbed the stairs with a heavy heart. Adah and Zillah were sleeping, blissfully unaware of all that had happened. Baby Annis stretched in her sleep, making little fists as Millie pulled the blankets up under her sweet, chubby chin. Millie found Don and Cyril cowering in the middle of Cyril's bed. The poor things had been there the whole time, not daring to peek downstairs.

"Are you going to yell at us, Millie?" Cyril asked.

"No, I won't yell," Millie said. "Can you tell me what happened?"

"We didn't mean for her to fall," Don said. "We didn't mean it . . ."

"We shouldn't have done it," Cyril said. "But we didn't know we shouldn't have until after we did. Not for sure."

"Shouldn't have done what?" Millie asked, sitting down on the corner of the bed.

"We were gonna throw snowballs at you and Ru when you came home. Aunt Wealthy wouldn't let us go outside," Don said.

"She wouldn't let us go out the doors," Cyril corrected. "I asked if we could go out the front door, and she said no.

So I asked if we could go out the back door. She said not to go out the front door, or the back door, or any of the windows," Cyril said. "But she never said not to go out the door into heaven."

Don't call it that! Millie wanted to yell. *I don't want my sister to go to heaven yet!* But she bit her lip instead.

"She never said that," Don agreed. "So we used Ru's hammer to get the nails out while Aunt Wealthy was downstairs, makin' hot milk for Annis."

They looked guiltily at each other, then Don went on. "Fan saw us. She said she was gonna tell if we didn't let her come with us, so we had to go right away, to keep her from blabbing. We were gonna climb down a rope, and we tied a real good knot—"

"I tied it," Cyril interrupted. "And Don went down first, then Fan. But she let go of the rope. She just let go."

"I didn't catch her," Don said. "When I saw her fall, I was afraid and I jumped back."

"I'm sure you couldn't have caught her," Millie said, rubbing his back. "Fan is almost as big as you are."

"She fell right on the ice on the street," Don said, his voice barely a whisper, "and she wouldn't get up. She screamed when she fell, and Pappa came running from nowhere. He picked her up and took her inside. And he just said, 'Go to bed, boys.' That's all. He didn't even let me help carry her," said Don tearfully.

"Don't be such a baby," Cyril said, punching his twin brother. "Fan's all right now. The doctor came and fixed her. And when Pappa comes up here, we are going to be in big trouble."

"No, dear," Millie said, surprised that her own tear-filled voice sounded as gentle as her mother's. "The doctor can't

fix Fan. We are asking God to do that now. Pappa and Mamma and Aunt Wealthy will stay with her tonight, and I will stay with you."

Don groaned. "I knew it was bad. I should've catched her, Millie. Pappa says to do what Jesus would do. Jesus wouldn't have let his sister fall." Don covered his head with his arms.

"I'm sure Fan forgives you," Millie said. "And Jesus forgives you, too."

"Did you ever kill somebody? Somebody who was your little sister?" Don sobbed. "Then don't say that. Mamma and Pappa must hate me now," he cried.

Jesus, what can I say to him? What can I do? "Shhhhhh," said Millie, putting one arm around each of her little brothers. "Of course they don't hate you. They will always love you, no matter what — just like I do. Let's talk to Jesus. Jesus, please help Fanny. Please heal her. Don't let her die. And help Don and Cyril. Their hearts are hurting."

"I'm sorry, God," Don said. "I'm so sorry."

Cyril was weeping silently, his shoulders shaking.

Millie pulled the quilt up to their chins and let the boys sob. They cried themselves to sleep in her arms. Only when their breathing was even and the sobs had stopped did Millie ease out carefully from between them. She took the stub of the candle she had left burning on the bedside table and hurried to her room to pick up her Bible and a new candle; then she returned to sit on the foot of Cyril's bed. Don was moaning in his sleep, and Millie rubbed his back until he quieted.

Lord, weren't You watching over Fan and Cyril and Don? Mamma and Pappa always pray for You to watch over us. Mamma always prays for guardian angels to surround her little ones. Did

they forget? Did You bring us to this horrible place so that Fan could die? Aunt Wealthy says that all things work together for the good of those who believe in God. Millie opened her Bible to Romans 8:28. *Yes. That's the verse Aunt Wealthy's always quoting: "And we know that in all things God works for the good of those who love him, who have been called according to his purpose." But how can this possibly be good? I don't understand, Lord. Weren't we called to Pleasant Plains according to Your purpose?*

CHAPTER

2

Special Gifts

Look at the birds of the air; they do not sow or reap or store away in barns, and yet your heavenly Father feeds them. Are you not much more valuable than they?

MATTHEW 6:26

Special Gifts

*T*he next morning, the scene in Celestia Ann's room had hardly changed. Marcia, Stuart, and Reverend Lord were praying, and Celestia Ann moved silently among them, taking care of every need.

"How is she?" Millie whispered from the doorway.

"The same," Celestia Ann replied, shaking her head. "But Reverend Lord is a powerful prayin' man, and your Mamma and Pappa are stormin' the gates of heaven itself for their little girl."

Aunt Wealthy came into the kitchen wearing her coat and Ru's boots as Millie was helping Celestia Ann set the breakfast table.

"Where are you going, Aunty?" Millie asked, surprised.

"Poor Belle needs milking," Aunt Wealthy said. "She can't wait for us to feel better."

"Is there anything I can do for you, Mamma?" Millie asked.

"Watch over your brothers and sisters," Marcia said. "That would be a tremendous blessing right now."

"I'll watch them 'til you get in," Celestia Ann said. "You go ahead and follow Aunt Wealthy outside."

"How did you know I wanted to talk with Aunty?" asked Millie.

"I just know things sometimes," Celestia Ann said, shrugging her shoulders.

Millie grabbed her coat and boots from the closet under the stairs, pulled them on, and hurried to the cowshed. She found Aunt Wealthy on the three-legged stool, her head leaned against Belle's side.

"It wasn't your fault that Fan fell," Millie said. "Don and Cyril told me the whole story."

15

Aunt Wealthy lifted her head. "Thank you for saying that, Millie. I know you are right. I feel like it's all my fault, but one thing I have learned in my walk with the Lord is that sometimes the way we *feel* has nothing to do with what is *true*. God is in control, no matter what we feel about it."

"If God is in control, why did He make Fan fall? How can we trust Him? I thought I was doing so well with the verse God gave me when we left Lansdale: 'Trust in the Lord with all your heart and lean not on your own understanding; in all your ways acknowledge him, and he will make your paths straight.' And now it's all come to pieces! If He lets terrible things like this happen, how can anyone trust Him?"

"Oh, Millie," said Aunt Wealthy, standing up and moving the pail of milk out of the reach of Belle's hooves. "There are some things we won't understand until we meet Him face to face. God didn't make Fan fall, although He did allow it. But we must trust Him," she said passionately. "We cannot give up hope — no matter what the doctor says."

"But what about Romans 8:28?" Millie asked. "'And we know that in all things God works for the good of those who love him, who have been called according to his purpose.' How could this possibly be good? I don't think the apostle Paul's little sister was dying when he wrote that."

"No," Aunt Wealthy said slowly, "his little sister was not dying. Someday you should read all of chapter eight at once, Millie. Too many people make the mistake of memorizing just that one verse. That chapter has seen me through some very rough times. During the almost fifty years I've been following the Lord, I've laughed and I've sung, but I've hurt a lot too. People I love have died —"

Millie put her hands over her face, but Aunt Wealthy's arms went around her instantly. "I don't mean that Fan is going to die. I don't know what God will do. But with the exception of Enoch and Elijah, nobody I know of has gotten out of this place without their body dying. God calls us to a wild adventure, not a tea party, my dear. I don't follow Jesus because He can give me a life without pain. I follow Him because He is *good*. Someday I will follow Him right through death, and into our Heavenly Father's house."

"I don't want Fan to die!" Millie sobbed against Aunt Wealthy's shoulder.

"Neither do I," Aunt Wealthy said, wiping Millie's tears with the corner of her apron. "And Reverend Lord is right. God has not answered our prayers yet with a yes *or* a no. Until He does, Millie, we just keep praying."

Aunt Wealthy carried the pail of milk back to the house and into the kitchen. Millie strained it through muslin mesh, and set it aside so that the cream could separate. *How can I do such normal, everyday things when Fan is so terribly hurt?* she asked herself. *But somebody has to do them. The household has to keep functioning. The children need their breakfast, and baby Annis needs to be changed.*

As soon as they heard what had happened, Adah and Zillah wanted to see their little sister. Millie led them to the kitchen corner where Fan lay and let them kiss their sister's brow. Then she ushered them from the room. Cyril kissed Fan, too, but Don stood pale and miserable against the curtain, watching his parents.

"Don, do you want to help Fan?" Millie asked. Don nodded mutely. "I think Fan would like it if you held her hand," Millie said.

Don walked slowly forward, eased down on the bed beside Fan, and slipped his hand into hers. Stuart put his arm around Don, and the little boy buried his face in his father's shoulder. "Can I stay, Pappa?"

"Yes, Don, I know Fan would like that," Stuart replied. "But the other children must go with Millie."

As Millie was skimming the cream from the milk, Claudina and Mrs. Chetwood arrived on the doorstep with a basket of food for the family. Mrs. Chetwood tried to persuade Marcia to eat and to drink some tea, but Marcia would not leave her child, or stop praying.

"I'm not leaving you, Millie," Claudina said as Mrs. Chetwood put on her own shawl and hat to leave. "Mother has given me permission to stay. I'll help you with the children."

Millie could not imagine running any kind of classroom on this day, so while Claudina dressed the children warmly, Millie wrapped baby Annis in a bunting, and they ushered the whole group out the front door.

"C'mon, Wannago," Cyril said. "You come with us." The pup laid his head on his paws and looked up at Aunt Wealthy.

"I think he wants to stay here today," Aunt Wealthy said, as Millie led the children out into the cold.

"Where are we going?" Adah asked.

"We can go to my house, Millie," Claudina said, "or to the Monockers'. They have plenty of room."

Millie didn't answer. She remembered what Dr. Chetwood's face had looked like last night when he was telling Pappa that Fan was going to die. She couldn't take the children there. And the Monockers . . . of course they would let the little Keiths — the little warehouse children — into their fine home, and look on it as an act of Christian

charity. But they would frown at Cyril if he stepped on a carpet, and "tsk, tsk" at Zillah and Adah's hair still in tousled braids, unbrushed from the night before. *Where do I go, Jesus? I need a friend who can just help. Just understand.* There didn't seem to be any clear answer, so Millie simply followed her feet where they took her — down the hill to the house behind the blacksmith's shop.

"Millie! Are we going to the Lightcaps'?" Claudina asked, alarmed. "Are you sure this is a good idea? Helen and Lu were saying the other day how wonderful it was that you visited the poor, just like it says in the Bible. But shouldn't we go somewhere . . . else?"

Millie paused for a moment and held Annis close for comfort. "I visit Rhoda Jane because she is my friend."

Claudina blushed, and she glanced at the open door of the smithy. The furnace was glowing inside, and Gordon Lightcap, in a leather smithy's apron, was pulling a horseshoe from the furnace with a pair of tongs. He hammered it against the anvil, *clang, tap, clang,* held it up to examine his work, and tossed it into a pail of water. Steam rose like a cloud around him.

"He doesn't look the same," Claudina said quietly. She had danced with Gordon at the Christmas Social the night before. Millie had to admit that Gordon didn't look as dashing in the smithy as he had in the mid-December moonlight, dressed in his father's old suit. "I just don't know if we should go over there . . . it might be . . ." Claudina unconsciously lifted the hem of her skirt. The ruffles on her Swiss lace pantalets almost covered her dainty shoes.

"Dirty?" Millie said. "They don't live in the smithy, you know, Claudina. They have a house. But you don't have to come with us." Millie started walking.

"Yes," Adah said, folding her arms. "You don't have to come." She followed Millie. Claudina stood for a moment, undecided, then ran after them. "Wait, Millie. You're right. Jesus had all kinds of friends, and He wasn't embarrassed by them. You Keiths are peculiar people, every one of you. You know that?" Claudina looked around curiously at the wooden steps and the rough exterior of the shabby frame house, as Millie knocked on the door.

"Why, Millie Keith!" Rhoda Jane said, opening it wide. "And Claudina!" She looked surprised. "What are you doing here at this time of the morning? And after such a late night at the Social, too," she exclaimed, laughing.

"There's been an accident," Millie explained. "Fan is seriously hurt, and I need to keep the children out from under foot."

"Come in out of the cold," Rhoda Jane said, drawing Millie and the others inside. "Ma has already gone to work, but I'm sure she wouldn't mind."

Emmaretta and Min stared big-eyed as the whole group crowded into the small house. Millie saw Rhoda Jane wince as Claudina's eyes took in the thin blankets, the table of rough boards, the chairs, and cook stove. Rhoda Jane's trundle bed was tucked under the bed where the little girls slept with their mother. Gordon's cot in the second room, a lean-to behind the stove, was neatly made. Claudina's eyes traveled from the bare floor to the curtainless windows — not even hesitating on the bookshelf — then dropped to her shoes as if she didn't know where to look or what to say.

Rhoda Jane's chin went up. "Would you like to take your coats off? It's warm in here."

"Yes, thank you," Millie said, unbundling Annis first and handing her to Rhoda Jane to hold while she took the coats

off the little girls. She briefly described the accident and Dr. Chetwood's visit. "Mamma and Pappa are praying now," she said. "And Reverend Lord and Aunt Wealthy."

"Is Fan going to get better?" Emmaretta asked.

"Shhhh, Em," Rhoda Jane said, taking all their coats and scarves and laying them on Gordon's cot. "We will talk about that later. Now what shall we do with our morning?" she asked, looking at the newcomers. "I don't suppose you all want to help Min and Emmaretta with their spelling?" The Keiths just stared at her with huge, sad eyes.

"We could work on the play," Emmaretta suggested. Was it only three days before that the children had been practicing the Christmas play that Zillah had written? Fan had insisted on being a shepherd just like Cyril and Don. Millie shook her head. No one had the heart to practice the play, as the missing shepherd was too much on their minds.

They were still undecided when Gordon came inside wearing his leather apron, his hands scrubbed red in the basin outside the back door. He was tall for seventeen, as tall as Stuart, and his arms were strong from working with the hammer all day.

"Good morning, ladies. I certainly enjoyed our dance last night, Claudina," Gordon said, bowing slightly. Claudina blushed. "To what do we owe this visit?" he asked. The twinkle went out of his eyes as Millie explained about Fan's accident. "Well, now, let's think." He fished a pocketknife and a piece of wood from his pocket and started to whittle.

"Gordy thinks with his hands," Rhoda Jane said, folding her arms. "If they aren't moving, his brain isn't working."

"My future's in my fingers," Gordon laughed, spreading his broad hand. "And a good thing, too, as I have no brain for books."

"That's because you don't try," Rhoda Jane said. "Honestly, Gordon, a boy your age should be able to read. You are setting a bad example for Emmaretta and Min."

Gordon just laughed again. His hands moved amazingly fast, and pale curlicues of wood fell like snow into the kindling box. The little Keiths watched in fascination as he put the finishing touches on the form of a bunny.

"They're praying for Fan, Gordy," Min said, not at all impressed with her brother's skill. "Her ma and pa are praying. Will that help her?"

Gordon blew the dust from his carving, then started to work on it again. "I don't know, pumpkin," he said, "but it can't hurt, can it? I think when I see the morning light up the day, like a stage set for a play, and a doe comes walking through the yard . . . I think that somebody must have made it all. Like a writer writes a play, or a blacksmith makes a horseshoe. If it's beautiful, there has to be some reason in it."

Rhoda Jane frowned. "What would Pa have said to that?" she asked.

Gordon held up his work, a sweet little bunny, and laughed. "Why, I expect he would have said, 'Good work, son! It looks just like a rabbit!' " He winked and tossed the newly made bunny to Zillah. "I know what to do now," he said. "Whittling always works. I think we should make a Christmas gift for our poor neighbors. Rhoda Jane and I make them a gift every year."

"You mean us?" Adah asked. "We're poor now 'cause we live in a warehouse."

"Oh, no!" Gordon laughed. "We have some neighbors who have no shoes!" He winked at his sister again, and she nodded.

22

"But they have coats!" Rhoda Jane said. "And some of them wear feathers, like an actress on a stage!"

"Mamma doesn't approve of actresses in feathers," Cyril said doubtfully.

"And they have no houses," Gordon said, ignoring Cyril's comment.

"But they do have homes!" Rhoda Jane said, laughing now. Millie began to smile at Gordon's humorous trickery.

Cyril shook his head. "I don't think I recollect them folks."

"I think you will know them when you see them," Gordon said. "We've been gathering the supplies for their Christmas present for weeks now! Will you help us?"

"I'll help," Zillah said.

Gordon produced a bushel basket of wrinkled, wizened apples. "Mrs. Prior donated these," he said, "because they are full of worms."

"Worms! Do poor folk eat worms?" Cyril asked.

"These folk won't mind," Gordon assured him, "if you are brave enough to slice the apples."

"I ain't afraid of worms!" Cyril said. Gordon produced his pocketknife, and Cyril set to work slicing the apples. He found no worms, as it was December, but worms had left their handiwork behind them; the apples were shot through with holes and brown powder. Gordon produced a needle and thread and got Emmaretta and Min started on stringing the apple slices.

"You ladies can help me," Rhoda Jane said, producing a kettle and a cup of corn kernels. She put the kettle on the stove and dropped in two spoonfuls of lard from the pot on the back of the stove. After the lard was sizzling, she poured in the corn, put the lid on tight, and shook the

pot. With the first ping of popping corn the kitchen filled with a delicious smell. When the popcorn was done, Zillah and Adah helped Emmaretta and Min string it on threads.

Millie's eyes went to the bookshelf. The Bible she had given Rhoda Jane was there, in between a volume of Shakespeare and a book of sonnets. Rhoda Jane hadn't burned it up after all, just set it on a shelf with all her other books. But if there were things in the Bible that not even Aunt Wealthy understood, could it possibly help Rhoda Jane, who had been hurt so badly?

Millie, Rhoda Jane, and Claudina took turns holding the baby or cracking nuts to mix with seeds and suet. They wrapped the sticky mixture around lengths of string.

When the string ornaments and garlands were done, Cyril shook his head. "Strange eatin' habits," he said. "I think I figured who these folks are."

"Strange indeed," Gordon laughed. "Come on, perhaps they will let us watch." They carried the decorations to the backyard and draped them on an evergreen tree.

"It's just as good as a Christmas tree!" Adah said. "Just as pretty."

"I was right!" Cyril said. "Folks with coats but no shoes!"

"Let's go watch from the window." Gordon led them back inside.

Rhoda Jane started tea while the children gathered around the window and waited.

"Look! The redcoats are coming!" Gordon said, as a cardinal arrived in a crimson flash. He was joined by other less stylish birds, crows in somber black and sparrows in monkish brown, and then a huge gray squirrel arrived, twitching his tail to let the birds know who was boss. Soon the tree was full of feasting creatures, some arguing loudly or grabbing a delicacy and leaping away.

Zillah leaned her head against the windowpane.

"What's wrong, Zil?" Millie asked.

"Fan would have loved this," she said. "Wouldn't she?"

"We'll do it again when she's up and around," Gordon said.

When they were finished watching the marvelous display, Gordon asked, "Who would like a ride on my new sled?"

Gordon, Ru, and Claudina led the children to the sled hill while Millie and Rhoda Jane cleaned the kitchen and watched over baby Annis. Later, they all had popcorn and potatoes fried in lard for dinner. Millie was sure that Mamma wouldn't approve of such a diet every day, but just now she was thankful to have the food.

When the shadows grew long, Millie knew she had to take the children home. She gathered them up, making sure they all had their coats and scarves and mittens.

"Thank you, Rhoda Jane," she said. "You have been such a help."

"Yes, it was wonderful," Claudina said politely. "I'm sorry I never visited you before. You must return my visit."

Rhoda Jane laughed. "What would your mother think? The washerwoman's daughter as a guest?"

Claudina flushed. "I'm sure she wouldn't mind." But she didn't sound sure at all.

"I'll come see you soon, Millie," Rhoda Jane promised.

The prayer vigil continued at the Keith house. Reverend Lord never seemed to move from his place, night or day. Neighbors and friends stopped by to express sympathy and

assure the Keiths of their prayers. Celestia Ann fed them tea and cookies and ushered them away.

Dr. Chetwood stopped in twice a day, examined Fan, and declared her unchanged. Millie was afraid she would lose a brother as well as a sister, for Don's face had grown pale, and he refused to eat or drink.

Late on the fourth day, Millie was rubbing her mother's shoulders when Aunt Wealthy gasped. "She moved! I saw her!"

Fan's eyelashes fluttered, and her blue eyes opened. "Hello, Reverend Lord," she whispered. "Were you the one who was singing so pretty?"

"Nobody was singing, kitten," Millie said.

"I'm sure they were," Fan said. "Pretty songs to Jesus. I'm thirsty."

"Of course you are!" Marcia was laughing, but tears were running down her face.

"Silly Mamma," Fan said, reaching up to touch a tear. "Why are you crying?"

"Oh, thank the Lord!" Aunt Wealthy said.

"Did Reverend Lord do something?" Fan asked.

"No," the reverend laughed. "But God did. He gave us a miracle!"

Celestia Ann brought tea for the convalescent, and when Fan held that down, she gave her chicken broth. Marcia allowed Fan to sit up for no more than a few moments, and all her brothers and sisters trooped in to see her.

When Dr. Chetwood arrived, he could only shake his head. "Unbelievable, simply unbelievable!"

"And just in time," Reverend Lord said. "If I had stayed much longer, I would have had no time to prepare my Christmas Eve sermon!"

Special Gifts

Celestia Ann brought the good reverend his coat, and he said his good-byes, promising to check in on Fan very soon. He slipped his arms into the sleeves and shook his shoulders to settle the coat, then looked bewildered at his wrists. The cuffs were no longer too short for his long arms. In fact, they fit perfectly.

"Good night and God bless," he said as he stepped out the door.

That evening the curtain that separated Celestia Ann's bed from the kitchen was removed, and the family gathered around Fan's bed to have dinner. Don was eating again, one bite for every sip that Fan took.

"Millie," Marcia whispered, "I can't tell you how proud I am of the way you took care of your brothers and sisters. You have grown up so much! Oh!" She put her hand to her mouth. "Millie, I forgot . . . you're thirteen today! It is today, isn't it?"

"Yes, Mamma," Millie laughed. "It's my birthday."

"*I* didn't forget," Celestia Ann said. "Cake's in the oven."

"Happy birthday, daughter!" Stuart said, picking her up in a bear hug. "We will have a proper celebration, and even a gift or two . . ."

"God gave me the best gift of all," Millie said, taking Fan's hand. "He gave me my little sister back."

⌇⟶⟩

"You carved this in a week? Gordon, it is simply amazing," Aunt Wealthy said, turning the angel this way and that to examine the detail. "You have God-given talent."

The small wooden angel held a sword defiantly aloft. Every fold of his cloak, every feather of his wings, stood out in perfect detail.

"I have had some time on my hands," Gordon said with a shrug. "Not too many folks need horses or mules shod at this time of year. Emmaretta and Min told me what to carve."

Fan was delighted with the fierce little warrior. She set him on the table by the door, where he could watch over the big family Bible with all their names inside.

"That angel is wonderful," Millie told Rhoda Jane. "I think that is just what they must look like."

"If they look like anything at all," Rhoda Jane said skeptically. "Gordy has carved fairies and unicorns for Emmaretta and Min . . . things that aren't real. He carved an angel because that's the kind of fairy story Fan likes."

"But, it's not just a story . . ." Millie began.

"Please, Millie, don't," said Rhoda Jane, her eyes full of shadows. "Fan is better, and I am so happy for you all. But . . ."

"What's wrong?" Millie put her arms around her friend. "What is it?"

"When my father was dying and Damaris brought me that Bible . . . I prayed, Millie. I prayed as if my heart would break . . . and Pa died. He died anyway. It's just chance, don't you see? Pa dies, and Fan lives. Just chance."

"But Rhoda Jane . . ."

Suddenly there was something fierce in Rhoda Jane's face. "You are my only friend in Pleasant Plains, Millie Keith," she said, "but it hurts too much to think about those things. Promise me you won't talk about God or the Bible anymore. I just can't take it!"

"I can't promise you that," Millie said slowly. "But I can promise that I will try not to. Not unless you ask me."

CHAPTER

3

True or False

For the ear tests words as the tongue tastes food.

JOB 34:3

*T*he Keiths caused quite a stir when they walked into church on Christmas Eve with Fan snuggled in Stuart's arms. People called it a Christmas miracle, as everyone in town had heard about Dr. Chetwood's diagnosis. Dr. Chetwood himself could not have been more delighted. Mr. Tittlebaum, the oldest member of Reverend Lord's flock, insisted on giving up his favorite spot on the front row for Fan. Wallace Ormsby and York Monocker used their coats to make cushions for the hard wooden bench, and Beth Roe joined Celestia Ann in waiting on Fan hand and foot. She sat like a golden-haired princess, adored by all.

Reverend Lord opened the service with a prayer of thanksgiving and praise, not just for Fan's recovery, but for the mercies and grace God showed every person in Pleasant Plains when He sent His Son to earth to be their Savior. After his sermon, the congregation sang carols and the ladies served spiced cider and Christmas cookies.

Millie took a moment to step aside from the group and stand on the far side of the room to watch her family and new friends and neighbors laugh and talk. How different this group of friends was from the one she had left in Lansdale. Helen and York Monocker, who formed the center of the group of laughing young people, would have looked at home in the finest parlor in Lansdale. Lu Grange, who was dressed almost as well, was at Helen's elbow, as always, nodding in agreement with everything she said. Beth Roe, dressed neatly in homespun clothes, listened from the outskirts of the circle. The young men, even those older than York — like Nicholas Ransquate —

followed York's lead when Gordon wasn't around. *Why, Celestia Ann is the prettiest girl here*, Millie realized. Celestia Ann's elfin features and merry laugh were turning heads and making even dowagers smile. *I wonder why I never noticed that before?* The little children ran and played among the adults who gathered in small groups discussing weather, politics, and news.

Not everyone was included in the lively discussion. Mr. Tittlebaum, who claimed to be twice as old as Moses, made his way across the room with the help of a hand-carved cane. Groups of people disappeared as he approached, like marbles scattering in slow motion. The old man had outlived two wives and all his children. Almost everyone in the room had been subjected to his endless stories of things that had happened before any of them were born.

Mr. Tittlebaum paused in the center of the room, turning around slowly. He stopped, his rheumy eyes fixed on the corner where Aunt Wealthy stood in an animated discussion with Mrs. Ormsby and Mrs. Prior.

Aunt Wealthy caught sight of his approach, and Millie saw her lift her eyes to heaven for just one moment; then Aunt Wealthy smiled and greeted him warmly as Mrs. Prior and Mrs. Ormsby hurried away.

Aunt Wealthy has more courage than anyone I have ever known, Millie thought. *Courage enough to face a lion, or even to spend an evening listening to poor Mr. Tittlebaum . . . A lifetime of adventure. That's what I want. But do I have enough faith to follow Jesus because He's good — no matter what happens? What if Fan had died? Would my faith have failed?*

Helen Monocker noticed Millie standing alone, and she started toward her, bringing her group of friends along like cork bobbers caught in the wake of a boat. She held out a

plate of cookies to Millie, white confections with a lace of sugar on top.

"You must try these, Millie," she said. "I baked them myself."

"They are beautiful, but no, thank you," Millie said politely.

"I insist," said Helen as she shoved the plate toward her. "Or is it true that you won't eat sugar because slave hands have touched it?"

Millie felt the heat creeping into her face. She was sure Helen never truly meant to offend, but her words were often harsh. It had taken her months to get used to Helen's abrupt manner. The first time Millie had had a heated discussion with Helen, she was surprised to find that the older girl had forgotten it the next day. Her opinions were strongly expressed and feebly held, and they tended to change with the weather.

"I believe slavery is wrong," Millie said. "I won't eat sugar because human beings who believe they own other human beings profit from the sale of sugar. Did you know that men, women, and children are worked to death on some plantations? And even on the best plantations they are kept against their will."

"So you are an abolitionist?" Helen's brother, York, asked in surprise. "My father says that abolitionists are troublemakers."

Jesus, Millie prayed quickly, *help me know what to say!* "I don't want to cause trouble," Millie said. "But I do want to do what's right. And I don't believe slavery is right. I cannot support it in any way."

"But don't you like sweets?" York asked.

"I do," Millie said, "but I use honey or maple sugar."

"Aren't you wearing cotton right now?" Helen asked. "That is a product of slave labor, is it not?"

"Not all of it," Millie said. "Mother is careful to buy from a mill that purchases only from free men."

"It doesn't seem to me that it would matter if one person ate a cookie," Wallace Ormsby remarked.

"That's true," Millie said. "But if God speaks to the hearts of ten thousand people, then it will make a difference."

"You believe God is speaking to your heart?" asked Damaris Drybread, the schoolmarm, joining the conversation.

If there had been a rug on the church floor, Millie would have happily crawled under it. Not only were the opinions of Damaris strongly held, but Millie often felt she had been beaten over the head when a conversation with the schoolmarm was over.

"If my heart is breaking over the things that break God's heart, how could He not be speaking to it?" asked Millie softly.

"And you are the judge of what breaks God's heart, Millie Keith?" Damaris persisted. "You take great pride in your Bible knowledge, it seems to me. Doesn't the Bible itself say that slaves should obey their masters? I assume you know the verse," Damaris continued. "It's in 1 Timothy 6:1: 'All who are under the yoke of slavery should consider their masters worthy of full respect, so that God's name and our teaching may not be slandered.' "

Millie sighed. Damaris had a great memory for Scriptures. "God is concerned about all human beings," Millie said. "Just because the Bible says that something exists doesn't mean that it is right. King David had more than one wife. You can't think that was right."

"Is that your own interpretation and commentary, or did you read it somewhere?" asked Damaris.

"It is my own," Millie said.

"So you would force the view of a twelve-year-old on the people in the Southern states?" the schoolmarm sniffed. Everyone was looking at Millie now. "I'm sure that none of them can read the Bible as well as you do, Millie."

Millie could feel her temper starting to rise. *Lord, help me be calm. Help me speak the truth in love like Mamma always does. Besides, I'm thirteen!* " 'An evil can seep through society'," she said, "and now I am quoting the *Liberator*, Mr. William Lloyd Garrison's abolitionist paper, 'so that even good people are blind to it. Then it is the responsibility of those who can see to speak out.' "

"And what do you 'see'?" Damaris demanded. "There is no commandment in the Bible that forbids owning slaves."

"Jesus said, 'Whatever you do for one of the least of these my brothers of mine, you do for me'," Millie said. "Would you chain Jesus in a work crew? Would you whip Him, and work Him to death so that you could have sweets, or cotton for your clothes? Or so you could live in a fine house while He lived in a dark shack? Wouldn't you consider anyone who did that to Jesus evil?"

"That is an entirely different thing," Damaris said. "Some people are born to that lot, and if they were not lazy, they would not be whipped."

"Wouldn't you think it was evil if you were the one being whipped or sold?" Millie looked around desperately. Claudina was surely on her side, but everyone seemed to be looking away, refusing to meet her eye. How could they sing carols one moment and refuse to stand up for the truth the next? She was feeling quite outnumbered, when her

mother caught her eye from across the room and started toward her, Fan in tow.

"Merry Christmas, Miss Drybread," Marcia said cheerily. "You have such a beautiful voice. I think we should start a choir."

Damaris was taken aback, but only for a moment. "Hello, Fan," she said. "I am glad to see you are better. It must have been terrifying falling out of that window."

Fan looked up at her and smiled. "I didn't fall," she said, "I jumped." Suddenly she seemed to catch sight of something in the distance. Her face froze with no expression, and her eyes were wide.

"Fan?" Millie said. "Are you all right?"

Fan didn't move, though Marcia shook her shoulder gently.

"Fan?"

Fan shivered from head to foot. "I jumped!" she repeated, as if there had been no pause in her conversation, and then looking up at her mother she finished, " 'cause the rope hurt my fingers. My head hurts now."

"What's wrong with her?" Damaris asked. "I thought there was a miracle."

"I expect she is overly tired," Marcia said, but her voice was worried. "It's time for the Keiths to be going home."

Damaris caught Marcia's elbow as the family started to walk away. "I hope you're resigned to what has befallen your child," she hissed. "You know you ought to be; we deserve all our troubles and trials."

"I do not think Fan did anything to deserve the fall," Marcia said. "She is hardly more than a baby."

"Perhaps she is not the one being punished," Damaris suggested. "Do you think you may have made an idol of

that child, Mrs. Keith? I think you have, for you pet and spoil all your children. God is jealous of your heart and won't allow idols, you know."

"We love all our children," Marcia said, "and we have never indulged them to their hurt."

"The heart is deceitful," the schoolmarm remarked.

"I trust Jesus has given me a new heart," Marcia said, "as He promised in Ezekiel — one that longs to serve Him. I know my heart is precious to Him, and yours is as well, Damaris. And I know my love for my children is precious to God, too. Thank you for your concern, Damaris."

"I'm only doing my duty," observed Damaris. "The Bible says that those who sin are to be rebuked publicly. Is pride not a sin?"

"It is. Merry Christmas, Damaris," Marcia said gently, gathering Fan in her arms and walking away. Millie followed her mother across the room, gritting her teeth. *How can anyone be so horrible?*

Stuart soon had the boys rounded up, and they said their good-byes. Millie kept a close eye on her sister as they walked home. *Is there something wrong with Fan? Why did she freeze like that?*

Deep winter had settled over Pleasant Plains. The air outside was cold enough to form ice crusts on the snow, and frost was deep on the windows. No one stirred from the houses if they could help it — everything and everyone seemed caught in changeless ice, and spring was an impossible thought.

The Keith family returned to their routine of school and chores, Millie and Ru taking lessons from Stuart, and

Millie in turn teaching her younger sisters, with special care taken for Fan, who was just learning her alphabet.

In the two weeks that had passed since Christmas, it had become obvious that something was wrong with the little girl. Sometimes she would freeze, unaware of her surroundings for moments at a time, and once in a while she fell to the floor shaking, remembering none of it when she got up. They didn't dare let her play alone near fire or water. If the shaking struck during a meal, whoever was closest would grab her cup and plate and move them away. All the Keiths watched her closely, keeping her from anything that could harm her. However, Fan was her old self most of the time, plaguing her brothers and twinkling her way into everyone's heart.

On one particular evening the Keith family had gathered in the kitchen, the warmest room in the Big Yellow House. Celestia Ann was preparing a sourdough starter for the next day's baking. Aunt Wealthy and Marcia were busy sewing curtains and draperies for the new house they would be moving into late in the spring. Ru was working on plans for the gardens and outbuildings. Stuart was reading a six-week-old newspaper from Chicago. The children were playing quietly on the rug, with Fan pretending to give milk to her doll.

Millie set down her quill. The nib needed trimming, for it was leaving blotches on her lesson plan that looked strangely like pirate ships, palm trees, and little Scottie dogs. Her mind drifted to daydreams of adventure somewhere warm and far away, but a sudden banging on the door jerked her upright.

"Who could that be at this time of night?" exclaimed Aunt Wealthy. It was only six o'clock, but the dark winter evening made it seem much later.

Ru went to answer the front door. Reverend Lord came back with him, the minister's nose bright red from the cold. He tripped on the corner of the carpet as he entered the room. He staggered, then he managed to right himself and hold out a hand to Stuart.

"Good evening, Mr. Keith," he said. "I was sitting at home and I suddenly started wondering how your little Fan was doing. I thought I might stop by and see. And . . . oh!" He seemed to realize he was clutching a book. "I brought along some reading."

"We are glad to have the company!" Stuart exclaimed, grasping his hand. "Won't you have a seat by the stove?"

Celestia Ann pulled up another chair, then went back to her baking. After discussing the weather and exchanging a few pleasantries, Aunt Wealthy suggested Reverend Lord read aloud from the novel he had tucked under his arm.

"If that would please everyone," Reverend Lord said, "I would be happy to." The children gathered around him. "*The Adventures of Solomon Tule, Mountain Man*," Reverend Lord began. "Chapter one . . ." Reverend Lord's voice was deep and pleasant, and Fan snuggled up contentedly in Aunt Wealthy's lap to listen.

Solomon Tule certainly had an interesting life. The end of chapter three found him completely submerged in the ice cold waters of a mountain lake, breathing through a reed while "death in moccasined feet" searched the shore.

"Ahem," Marcia said.

Reverend Lord closed the book.

"No!" Don said. "You can't stop! He's gonna freeze if you leave him there!"

"Won't you keep reading?" Zillah pleaded.

Reverend Lord looked at Marcia.

"It's late, my dears," she said, "and my children must have their sleep. Perhaps Reverend Lord will come back tomorrow night?"

"I'd be happy to," the reverend said. "And I will leave the book here so I will not be tempted to read ahead."

"Awww, Mamma, can't he read more tonight?" Cyril begged.

"The bricks are just hot enough to chase off the shivers," Celestia Ann said, opening the oven and touching one of the bricks she had set inside. "We don't want them much hotter than this."

"That means it's bedtime," Stuart said. "I don't want my children to have toasted toes."

Millie smiled. Marcia might have been persuaded, but Stuart had spoken. The younger children kissed their parents. Ru, Cyril, and Don shook hands with Reverend Lord, and Aunt Wealthy led them off to bed. Celestia Ann followed them up the stairs, carrying the bucket of bricks. While the children changed into their nightshirts she would wrap a brick in a towel and tuck it between the sheets at the foot of each bed to drive out the chill.

Millie was now allowed to stay up with the adults, and she enjoyed the company and conversation every night. This evening the talk turned to Scripture, then to world events, and finally to God's plans for Pleasant Plains. When Reverend Lord spoke of his church, his face lit up. He was most animated when discussing the piano fund. It had no money in it at present, but Mrs. Ormsby had donated a cow. It was a thin, pathetic creature, to be sure, but Reverend Lord was attempting to fatten it by means of copious prayer and extra helpings of corn. His plan was to sell her when she grew fat. Unfortunately, the expense

of the corn—which came from his own meager living allowance—was starting to mount, the cow was no fatter, and now, if he sold her for her hide, he would not recover his expenses.

"You can always eat her yourself," Aunt Wealthy said kindly, "if you run out of food."

"I can hardly bear the thought," said Reverend Lord. "When she looks at me with those big trusting eyes, I simply go to town and buy another bag of corn."

As the clock was chiming nine, Reverend Lord rose, bid them all goodnight, and started his long walk home.

He appeared the next night promptly at six. On the third night Celestia Ann had saved dessert, and they all ate it together. It became apparent that a new tradition was being born. Reverend Lord had a very good education, and once he became comfortable with the Keith family, they found it as fascinating to hear him talk as it was to hear him read. Everyone looked forward to his knock on the door, and if he had to visit a member of his church who was sick or needed counsel, he was missed by the whole family.

Aunt Wealthy took an interest in the piano fund, and she contributed a small amount each week in the form of a bag of corn for Reverend Lord's cow. She would often stop by the cowshed to "check on the piano." She'd pat the cow's nose, examine its bony hide, and pray over it.

"I never heard of no cow named Piano," Mr. Tittlebaum said one day at church when Aunt Wealthy explained her mission. But the name had stuck, and Stuart had many a chuckle at what he referred to as "the musical moo."

Millie's Courageous Days

One bright morning when Millie rang her school bell to call her students to class, Celestia Ann was rolling out a pie crust on a pastry fabric on the table. Millie waited for her to finish before placing Adah and Zillah's slates on the table. Fan, who had been allowed to attend the class since Christmas, couldn't wait for a slate. She used a finger to draw letters on a fine powder of flour that had fallen on the table. "Look, Millie," she said. "I can spell cat!" Her chubby finger carefully traced out the letters D-O-G.

"That doesn't spell cat," Millie corrected her. "It spells dog."

"No, it doesn't! Celestia Ann says it spells cat. It says cat, doesn't it, Celestia Ann?"

Celestia Ann pointed at the letters one at a time and read: "C-A-T. Cat," she agreed, smiling at Millie.

"Whatever gave you that idea?" Millie said. "Look. She pulled out Fan's *McGuffey's First Reader* and turned to the picture of a cat. "See? These letters are C-A-T. They spell cat."

"Well, I'll be hornswoggled," Celestia Ann said. "I wonder how that happened?"

CHAPTER

4

Learning Soup

Let the word of Christ dwell in you richly as you teach and admonish one another with all wisdom.

Colossians 3:16

Learning Soup

*E*ven before she knocked on the Lightcaps' door, Millie heard the noise inside. "Come in, Millie!" Emmaretta called, opening the door. "I saw you coming."

Millie stepped inside. Mrs. Lightcap and Rhoda Jane were dancing around and around the room, stomping and shouting.

"What on earth is going on here?" Millie laughed, as Min and Emmaretta grabbed her hands and twirled her around.

"Your father is a great man, Millie Keith," Rhoda Jane said, curtsying to her.

"That is true," agreed Millie. "Is this dance in his honor?"

"Yes," said Mrs. Lightcap, brushing a strand of hair from her face. "Actually, it is."

"Mr. Grange called Ma into the bank," Rhoda Jane said. "Did you know that the stagecoach road to Pleasant Plains will be completed this spring?"

"I did not."

"Well, it will. And they will have to have a way station here for the stagecoaches. They will need someone to work as a hostler to keep the horses, and someone to run the rest of the station."

"What has that got to do with Pappa?"

"He planned and arranged the whole thing," said Rhoda Jane. "The stagecoach company is donating the lumber for a livery stable that'll be built on the property between your house and ours. Gordon will be the hostler, and he will shoe the horses. The station will also have a kitchen, eating area, and rooms for guests which Ma and I will take care of."

"Where will that be?" asked Millie.

"At the Big Yellow House once your family moves out," Mrs. Lightcap explained.

"That's wonderful!" said Millie. "You won't have to do laundry anymore!"

"I am baking the Keiths a cake to say thank you!" Mrs. Lightcap exclaimed, then she clapped her hands over her mouth. "The cake! Shhhhh! Children, shhhhh! The cake will go flat!"

She tiptoed to the oven, grabbed a towel, and opened the door. The cake wasn't flat at all. It bulged upward at the edges and collapsed into a great trough in the middle.

"Oh, dear," she said mournfully, pulling it out of the oven.

"I'm so sorry," Millie said. "Perhaps it was the stomping."

"No," Emmaretta said, "Ma's cakes always look like that."

"Sometimes they don't rise around the edges," Min added helpfully. "And sometimes they just get flat in the middle."

"Maybe I should have told Mr. Grange that I can't cook," Mrs. Lightcap said.

"Ma," Rhoda Jane said, taking the towel from her mother's hand, "he didn't ask if you could cook. He asked if you *wanted* to cook."

"That's true, but . . ."

"I'll do the cooking," Rhoda Jane said. "Maybe we'll get a piano, and you can sing."

"I didn't know that you could sing," Millie said in surprise.

"Oh, yes," Mrs. Lightcap said, striking a dramatic pose. "I have been on the stage in London . . . Rome . . ."

"You have been to England and Italy?" Millie asked in astonishment.

"Not really," Mrs. Lightcap laughed. "It was New London, Connecticut, and Rome, New York. But I *was* on the stage. That's how I met Mr. Lightcap. He was wonderful as Hamlet."

"You met Pa on top of a stage?" Min asked. "Like the one that's coming to Pleasant Plains?"

"No, dear. Quite another kind of stage."

"Do you know what this means?" Rhoda Jane asked, coming back to the subject at hand. "We'll have newspapers less than six weeks old! Practically hot off the press. Can you imagine? We'll know what's happening in Chicago almost as soon as it happens!"

Millie laughed. The only newspapers in Pleasant Plains were the ones Stuart ordered from Chicago. They came by ship across the Great Lakes, then by boat up the St. Joseph River, just like the Keiths had when they moved to Pleasant Plains. Rhoda Jane always awaited them almost as eagerly as did Stuart himself.

"Of course, I'll still have to wait until the whole Keith household reads them before you pass them on."

"Not the whole household," Millie said. "Fan can't read yet, and neither can Celestia Ann." She told the story of the morning's spelling lesson.

"Doesn't Celestia Ann read at all?" Rhoda Jane asked, dumping her mother's cake in the slop bucket. "She has such a good mind."

"No," said Millie, unwrapping the molasses cookies she had brought to share and handing one each to Min and Emmaretta. "And it's a pity. I distinctly remember Aunt Wealthy offering to teach her to read last fall. Celestia Ann

said that no book ever helped her milk a cow, or scrub a floor, for that matter."

"Then why would she care how you spell cat?" Rhoda Jane asked, helping herself to a cookie. "And what could have given her the idea that D-O-G spells cat?"

"I have my suspicions," Millie said. "And it was a who, not a what."

"Something must have piqued her interest in reading."

"She used to tell stories to the children in the evening," Millie said, dipping her cookie in the cup of milk Rhoda Jane handed her. "But now that Reverend Lord is reading, she almost never says a word."

"Reverend Lord, eh?" Mrs. Lightcap's right eyebrow went up. "Hmmmmmmm," she muttered with an unusual twinkle in her eyes.

"Ma!" exclaimed Rhoda Jane.

"You don't think Celestia Ann likes — " Millie began, as half of her cookie fell into the milk.

"Never mind," Rhoda Jane interrupted.

While Millie fished for the soggy cookie, her mind raced back over the last few weeks. She remembered Celestia Ann standing by Reverend Lord's side as he faced the doctor; Celestia Ann kneeling by his side as he prayed for Fan; Celestia Ann sitting in the shadows, listening as he read. And how exactly had Reverend Lord's coat sleeves grown longer as he prayed over Fan? How indeed!

"Would you mind if I join you for the reading tonight?" Rhoda Jane asked Millie. "I think some investigation is in order," she said with a wink and a smile.

That evening Rhoda Jane sat in the Keiths' living room with Reverend Lord and Celestia Ann. Rhoda Jane seemed

to enjoy the reading as much as anyone else, but Millie saw her steal a look at Celestia Ann now and then.

What do people look like when they are in love? Millie wondered. *How can you tell? Celestia Ann doesn't look any different than she did last week, and if she is paying special attention to anyone, it certainly isn't to Reverend Lord. She smiled at him when she served chamomile tea after dessert, but she smiled even more brightly at Cyril.*

While everyone had tea, Celestia Ann sat quietly in the corner. The reading continued for a little while until it was interrupted by a snort. "Cyril, are you all right?" Aunt Wealthy sounded alarmed.

Cyril did not look well. His face was red, his eyes were watering, and his lips were puckered up.

"Are you all right?" Reverend Lord asked, setting his book down. Cyril leaped from his chair and rushed out the back door.

"What on earth?" Marcia wondered, starting to rise, but before she did, Cyril was back.

"Pardon my exit," he said glaring around the room, "but spittin' in public ain't polite."

"Isn't polite," Stuart corrected.

"That's right, it isn't," Cyril agreed. "Even when somebody puts salt in your tea instead of honey!"

"Well, I'll be hornswoggled," Don said, looking across the room at Celestia Ann, who smiled sweetly, set down her sewing, and offered to fetch Cyril a new cup of tea.

"No, thanks," Cyril said, "I'll get it my ownself."

"Oh, I couldn't let you," Celestia Ann assured him, standing up. "Why, the cups are up so high that if you toppled one it would be a cat-astrophe, don't you think?"

"Dog-gone if it wouldn't," Cyril said, folding his arms and looking her dead in the eye.

Rhoda Jane exchanged a look with Millie. Everyone else was looking from Cyril to Celestia Ann, but they were giving away no more.

Celestia Ann took a cup from the shelf beside the stove, and Cyril watched her carefully as she poured the tea and stirred in a generous spoonful of honey. "There," she said. "That oughta be enough to sweeten *anything* up."

Celestia Ann sat back down, looking like an angel with a curly red halo. Millie couldn't help but wonder if angels ever had that *particular* glint in their eye.

After the little children were put to bed, conversation turned to the Lord, as it generally did. "The more people in Pleasant Plains who act as Jesus would have acted, the more this town will change," Aunt Wealthy remarked.

"I agree," said Reverend Lord, nodding. "Church attendance increased after people heard about Fan. But when they compliment my sermon, I'm afraid they have just come to be entertained. Church is supposed to be so much more than that."

"Just be faithful in preaching the Word and living what you preach," Stuart said. "You are planting the seeds, but only God can make them grow."

"That's one of the reasons I enjoy spending my evenings here," Reverend Lord declared. "Your whole house feels like church—you know, the way church should really be. Not just wearing our best clothes and putting on our Sunday smiles, but living like Jesus."

Millie tried hard not to look at Rhoda Jane, but she could see that her friend was fidgeting. *Lord, plant Your seeds in Rhoda Jane's heart!*

"Thank you, Reverend Lord," Stuart said. "That is a great compliment. And I'll let you in on our secret, in case you ever want to start a family of your own."

He took the big family Bible from the shelf and turned to Psalm 15. "I have prayed these verses over my family for years."

"Lord, my desire is that we as a family dwell in Your sanctuary and live on Your holy hill. Let it be true of each of us that our walks are blameless and that we do what is righteous in Your eyes; that we speak the truth from our hearts, and have no slander on our tongues; that we do our neighbors no wrong and cast no slur on our fellow men; that we despise those who do evil, but honor those who fear You. Help us to keep our oaths, even when it hurts; and may we not be greedy or ever accept a bribe against the innocent. May we be constant in these things so that we will not be shaken. In the name of Christ Jesus our Lord and Savior, Amen."

They all sat in silence, allowing Stuart's prayer to settle in their hearts. Then Stuart added, "That is the kind of individuals I asked God to make us, and the kind of home I want to have. 'As for me and my household, we will serve the Lord,'" said Stuart, quoting Joshua 24:15.

"We like to think," Marcia said softly, "that Jesus is not just a guest in our house, but that He lives here."

"That explains why I sense His peace in this home," said Reverend Lord.

Millie sneaked a look at Rhoda Jane, and saw in her face that she was uncomfortable. *Rhoda Jane won't go to church. But we can bring Jesus to her!*

"Oh, dear, look at the time," Rhoda Jane said, standing up. "I need to be going. It was so nice of you to allow me to spend the evening, Mr. and Mrs. Keith."

"We love having you over, Rhoda Jane," responded Marcia, rising to see her to the door.

Rhoda Jane was quiet as Millie and Ru walked her home. Ru carried the lantern pole. The shade captured the light, directing it downward and forming a puddle of light on the snow just large enough for the three figures if they walk close together. A few yards from the doorstep, Millie turned to Ru.

"Would you mind waiting here for me?" she asked. "I want to speak with Rhoda Jane."

Ru rolled his eyes. "Go ahead, but I'm keeping the lantern."

Millie and Rhoda Jane walked through the darkness toward the splash of light spilling out of the window.

"Well? What do you think?" Millie asked when they were out of earshot.

"You said you weren't going to ask me about religion," Rhoda Jane said accusingly. "You promised."

Millie looked at her blankly. "I meant about Celestia Ann and Reverend Lord."

"Oh, that!" Rhoda Jane relaxed, and she looked a little sheepish. "I can't tell. Is it a sign of love if Celestia Ann poisons Cyril right in front of everyone?"

"It wasn't poison," Millie giggled. "It was salt."

"That's true."

Millie shook her head. "I can't tell, either."

"I think I'll have to watch them a little longer," Rhoda Jane said thoughtfully. "If Ma allows, may I come over tomorrow night?"

"Of course," Millie said calmly, but her heart leaped up. Rhoda Jane was coming back! She hadn't been frightened away.

"Perhaps Celestia Ann has just fallen in love with books," speculated Rhoda Jane, "and not Reverend Lord at all."

"That may be it," Millie agreed. "But really, I don't care why Celestia Ann wants to learn to read. I think it's wonderful, and I'm going to help her."

"Of course you are, Millie Keith," Rhoda Jane said. "Goodnight."

And so both Millie's classroom and the group in the Keiths' kitchen every evening grew by one. Celestia Ann took brief breaks from her work to learn with Millie, and within a few days she was reading simple words. Millie explained the project to her mother and aunt, and they were both eager to help.

As for Celestia Ann, she applied herself with the same energy she applied to any chore, and Millie was amazed at how quickly the young woman learned.

"I already knew what the words *sound* like," Celestia Ann explained. "I just didn't know what they *look* like. Once you know the first part of a sentence, it's kinda easy to figure out what the next part will say."

Marcia and Aunt Wealthy spent more and more time with Celestia Ann in lively discussions of political, historical, and spiritual topics, and Rhoda Jane dropped by occasionally in the afternoons with a book of children's poems to read aloud.

"Emmaretta and Min learned poetry quickly," she told Millie later. "Because the words rhyme, it's easy to learn what they are."

"I know what you all are up to," Celestia Ann said one day when she was alone with Millie. "You're makin' learnin' soup," she laughed, "all around me, so I just sort of drink it up!"

An Unexpected Guest

God sets the lonely in families.

PSALM 68:6

An Unexpected Guest

*T*he Keiths were living closely together inside the Big Yellow House that winter. It was too cold to be outdoors for long, so the family stayed within the four warehouse walls, private areas separated only by curtains.

Millie thought longingly of her swing across town atop the Keith hill, where the shell of their new house was waiting to be finished. The lot had been fenced in almost as soon as Stuart purchased it, and workers were hired to dig the cellar and put up walls. It had been roofed in before the first heavy snowfall, and work continued inside with laying wood floors, lathing, and hanging doors.

"Millie Keith," said Aunt Wealthy one day, pointing at Millie with her umbrella. "You seem awfully quiet today. What you need is a good walk. Would you like to come with us?" Aunt Wealthy and Wannago spent a good hour walking every day. Rain or shine, Aunt Wealthy could be seen carrying her purple umbrella with Wannago trotting at her heels. Aunt Wealthy loved her solitude and her talks with God. Millie had never before been asked along.

"I would love to come!" exclaimed Millie.

Aunt Wealthy was warmly, if colorfully, dressed for her walk in a purple cloak and a gold-and-purple turban. Millie had asked her once why she dressed up to go on her prayer walks, and Aunt Wealthy had laughed. "I like to put my best foot forward when I am walking with the Lord," she said. "I have had the most marvelous adventures on my walks, and I like to be prepared for any occasion!"

Millie hurried to get her coat and scarf, pulling them on as she followed Aunt Wealthy out the door into the dazzling white world. It had snowed again in the night, two inches of fresh powder over the hard crust of old snow. The boughs of the evergreens were iced but not drooping with snow. Wannago yapped, and the white blanket on the world muffled the sound, making him seem far away from them. "Lord, what a glorious day You have created!" Aunt Wealthy prayed aloud. "Thank you!"

Aunt Wealthy led the way, taking the path to the top of the hill. The boys had been sledding the day before, but the new powder made the path fresh, not a footprint in sight. Millie followed in Aunt Wealthy's steps, and last of all was Wannago, leaping and rooting in the snow with his nose.

When they reached the top, Aunt Wealthy spread her arms, closed her eyes, and smiled. Millie couldn't help but smile with her, only partially because the peacock feather bobbing in Aunt Wealthy's turban gave her the appearance of a tropical bird who had lost its way.

"Listen to that!" Aunt Wealthy exclaimed suddenly. "Isn't it marvelous!"

Millie turned her head, listening for the sound, but everything was winter silent. Even the clang of Gordon's hammer was still.

"I don't hear a thing."

"That's what's so marvelous. Solitude!"

Millie looked at her aunt's peaceful face, which was upturned toward the sun. How hard it must be for her to live in a house full of children, with curtains for walls. Sound carried right through the fabric, and from the moment the Keiths had set foot in the warehouse, the only quiet times had been when the children were in bed asleep.

"Thank you for asking me to come with you," Millie said.

"You looked as if you could use some solitude yourself," Aunt Wealthy smiled. "I find it much easier to talk to God when I am all alone."

That was it exactly. On their journey to Pleasant Plains they had spent some weeks aboard a canal packet, sharing one cabin with all the passengers and crew. It was very hard to never be alone. The Big Yellow House was just the same, Millie realized. Because of the constant noise, one never had the sense of being alone.

"How do you manage?" Millie asked. "You were used to having your own house . . . now to be part of such a large crowd, in a house with fabric walls."

"A large, noisy crowd!" Aunt Wealthy laughed. "But it's not so bad, really. The children of Israel lived in tents for forty years, remember? They had to listen to each other, and to their neighbors as well."

At that moment, Wannago barked.

"What is it?" Aunt Wealthy said, turning to see what the fuss was all about.

The pup had found Ru's sled beneath a bush. Gordon's and Cyril's sleds were with it.

"He was sledding yesterday with the boys," Millie said laughingly. "I expect he wants a ride."

Wannago barked and looked eagerly at Aunt Wealthy.

"Don't be ridiculous," Millie told the dog.

"I don't think it's ridiculous at all," Aunt Wealthy said, examining the sleds. "I don't suppose the boys would mind if we used them? I haven't had any excitement for some time."

She picked up Gordon's sled and tapped the steel runner with her umbrella. "I expect this one will really go!"

Millie's Courageous Days

Millie looked down the sled hill. The boys had piled heaps of snow on it to make their sleds jump. The sled path crossed the road and ended in a huge snowbank.

"Let's race," Aunt Wealthy said. "Choose a sled."

"Are you sure . . ." Millie began.

"Pish-tosh," Aunt Wealthy said, pulling the sled to the edge of the hill. "You have been doing very well with all your work, Millie. You teach your sisters and do well in your own lessons, as well as help your Mother around the house. But life is supposed to be fun, too. If it's not against God's law and not opposed to man's law either, why not try it? He gave us a whole universe to explore! Why would He have created snowy hills if He didn't want us to race down them on sleds?"

"Ru says that Gordon's sled is the fastest," Millie said.

"Would you like to use that one?" Aunt Wealthy asked. "I'll choose another, if it will make the race more fair."

"No, thank you, Aunty." Millie chose Ru's toboggan, and set it next to Aunt Wealthy's sled. Aunt Wealthy gathered her skirts and petticoats and pulled her feet up onto the sled. She draped her umbrella over her arm, and Wannago jumped up behind her. Millie settled herself on the toboggan.

"Are you ready?" asked Aunt Wealthy.

Millie nodded.

"Set? Go!" Aunt Wealthy shoved off with her umbrella. Millie tried to push off with her heels, but the toboggan floundered in the new snow powder. Not so with Gordon's steel runners. They cut through the powder to the hard-packed snow beneath. Aunt Wealthy was moving unbelievably fast when she reached the first hill. She gave a startled whoop as the sled took to the sky. Wannago flew into the air, tumbling head over heels when he landed, but by that time, Aunt Wealthy was long gone, flying over the

second hill and heading for the road. Millie gasped. The road! There was a horse and cart just rounding the bend.

"Stop, Aunty!" Millie yelled. "Throw yourself off!"

If Aunt Wealthy heard the warning, it was too late. She shot into the road. The horse reared, and Aunt Wealthy streaked past, right under the horse's hooves. The sled hit the soft snow on the other side and stopped abruptly. Aunt Wealthy did not — she catapulted head first into the deep snow.

"Aunty!" Millie cried, and she started running and sliding down the hill. Wannago, who seemed unhurt, raced to Wealthy.

The cart had stopped, and a short, round farmer jumped out and tried to calm the horse, which was crow-hopping in between kicks. "Are you all right?" Millie yelled, arriving just as Aunt Wealthy crawled out of the snowbank.

"Quite. Oh, my!" said Aunt Wealthy, with a shimmy. "Eeek!" She started jumping up and down. "I seem to have gotten snow in my corset. Oh! Pardon me!"

The farmer had gotten his horse under control and was standing behind Millie. Millie was not sure if the shocked look on his face was the result of Aunt Wealthy's wild ride, her bouncing up and down to shake out the snow, or the mention of her under-things.

"You gave me a fright, lady," he said. "Are you all in one piece?"

"Yes, thank you," Aunt Wealthy said. "I do apologize for frightening your horse."

"I expect you just startled him awake," the fellow said, "comin' like a banshee outta nowheres like that. The cold is making even me sleepy."

Millie noticed for the first time that he wasn't wearing an overcoat, just a heavy shirt.

Aunt Wealthy asked, "Have you come a long way, Mr. — ?"

"Rose," the gentleman said, offering her his hand. "Bartholomew Rose."

"As I was asking, Mr. Tulip," Aunt Wealthy said, "has your journey been long?" They walked back toward the wagon.

"Rose," Millie whispered, but the farmer didn't seem to notice Aunt Wealthy's mistake.

"I come a far piece," he said. "But I have a delivery to make. Couldn't wait."

They reached the wagon and he pointed to a buffalo robe.

"You are delivering a buffalo robe," Aunt Wealthy said curiously. "Why don't you just wear it? Surely it would keep you warm."

He reached down and pulled back the robe gently. A baby, perhaps six months old, was sleeping on a pile of hay. Her face was dirty, and her hair was so matted that the color was uncertain.

"Mandy Rose," he said. "A consumin' cough carried her folks away, and her older brother as well. I'd keep her if I had a missuz, but she'd be better off with womenfolk, I imagine. I brung her to Pleasant Plains."

"The poor darling!" Aunt Wealthy said, touching the baby's cheek. "I don't recall a family of Tulips in town!"

"Roses," Millie corrected.

The farmer shrugged. " 'Taint surprisin'. I'm lookin' for someone by the name of Drybread. Damaris Drybread."

CHAPTER

6

A Crying Shame

And whoever welcomes a little child like this in my name welcomes me.

MATTHEW 18:5

A Crying Shame

s it far now to the Drybread place?" asked Mr. Rose.

"A good way still," Aunt Wealthy replied, "but our house is just around the corner. If you are willing we can warm you and the baby up, and send for Damaris. Does she know you are coming?"

"Nope," said the farmer, after accepting the offer of warmth gratefully. "I'm no hand at writin'."

They soon pulled up in front of the Big Yellow House, and Mr. Rose looked at the baby uncertainly.

"May I carry her?" asked Millie.

"I wished you would," he said. Millie gathered the baby in her arms. Aunt Wealthy opened the door and ushered them all inside.

"What's that, Millie?" Fan asked, jumping up from her seat.

"A baby," Millie said. "Smaller than Annis. Her name is Mandy Rose, and she's come a long way in the cold."

"Oh, let me see her, Millie," Zillah said, rushing over.

"Me, too!" burst out Fan, standing on tiptoe to get a better look.

"Ru," called Aunt Wealthy, "would you take care of Mr. Tulip's horse and wagon? They are standing in the road."

"Yes, ma'am," replied Ru as he left.

"Can I hold her, Millie? Please?" asked Fan.

The commotion woke Mandy Rose, and she opened her big blue eyes to look around her.

"Hi, baby," Fan said, giving her a kiss. Mandy Rose smiled, producing dimples in each cheek, and held out dirty hands to Fan.

"Now, hold on one minute!" Celestia Ann said.

"Yes," Don said, grabbing Fan by the apron strings and dragging her back. "You don't know where that baby's been. She looks dis-rep-utable to me." He glared at Mr. Rose. "This whole sitcheation appears dis-rep-utable."

"That's not what I meant," Celestia Ann said, laughing. "I meant you can't hold her by yourself, Fan. She's too heavy. We'll put a blanket on the floor for you both. And I expect she'll want some food." She pulled a blanket off her bed in the next room and spread it on the floor.

"Well, now, that's fine," Mr. Rose said, warming his hands over the stove. Aunt Wealthy excused herself, going upstairs to change out of her snowy, wet clothes. Mr. Rose finished with his hands, turned his backside to the stove, and lifted his shirttail to heat the seat of his pants. He seemed perfectly content to let the Keiths and Celestia Ann care for the baby.

Millie found a bottle and rubber nipple of Annis's. Celestia Ann filled the bottle with milk and set it in a pan of water to heat while Millie kept a close eye on Fan and Mandy Rose. The baby took the bottle eagerly, and Millie let Fan hold it for her.

"Eeuuuw," Don said, pinching his nose. "This baby smells bad."

"She don't smell bad," Cyril said. "She plum stinks."

"Needs changing, I expect," Mr. Rose said. "I had her since yesterday, and I don't got baby fixins. Fed her some soft cheese, though."

"I've got warm water," Celestia Ann said. "That child needs a bath."

"Whose baby is she, Millie?" asked Adah.

"Well," Millie said, glancing at Mr. Rose, "she's . . . Damaris Drybread's baby."

The children looked at one another in dismay.

"You all know her?" the farmer asked.

"Yes, sir," Zillah said. "She's the schoolmarm."

"A schoolmarm! Well, that's fine! That'll work out just fine for little Mandy. Now, if you'll just give me my coat, I'll be on my way."

"Wait!" Millie said. "You can't just leave her. Don't you need to speak to Miss Drybread?"

"No, Miss," the farmer said. "You folks seem to be doin' a good job here. I expect you'll figure out what to say."

"At least leave a letter of explanation," Millie said desperately.

"No time." He put on his hat. "Been nice meeting you, though."

Millie was trying to figure out a way to detain him when Aunt Wealthy reappeared. "Surely you are not going, Mr. Periwinkle?"

"It's Rose, lady. Rose! And I gotta go." He grabbed his coat and escaped through the door.

"Now what are we going to do about you?" Millie asked, tickling the baby's chin.

"She can't tell us, Millie," Cyril said. "She's too little."

"That's true," Millie said. "Don, did Mr. Rose leave the door open? There's a draft."

Don went into the front room, and came back dragging Fan by the hand. "You can't go following strangers outdoors!" he said.

"He wasn't a stranger," Fan said. "I liked him."

"He dropped a dirty baby on us," Ru said. "You can't get much stranger than that."

Millie sent Zillah and Adah in search of clothes and nappies for the baby. She stripped off the baby's soiled, crusted

clothing, and Don, after some persuasion, carried it to the trash heap.

The little girl's skin was red with rash under her nappies, and she cried when Millie set her in the water, but she soon cheered up as the warmth soaked in. Aunt Wealthy set to work making a salve of sweet oil and slippery elm for her rash. "It's been some time since we've needed this recipe," said Aunt Wealthy.

Millie had bathed Annis many times, and she knew how to lean Mandy Rose back just far enough to lather her hair. The little Keiths all gathered around to watch as Millie washed layer after layer of dirt away.

"She's a good little one," Celestia Ann said. "And she might be pretty, too, if she wasn't so thin."

By the time Marcia and Stuart arrived home, Mandy Rose was clean and sweet-smelling. Her hair, which turned out to be black, fell in curls around her little face. Her blue eyes were huge and solemn as she gazed up at Marcia.

"The precious thing!" exclaimed Marcia, picking her up.

"And that Mr. Rose left," Celestia Ann said indignantly. "Just dropped the baby off and left."

"I tried to get him to write a letter to Miss Drybread, but he wouldn't," said Millie.

"If the family name is Rose instead of Drybread, the mother must have been Damaris's sister. This will likely come as quite a shock. She might not have known her sister was ill."

"Mamma, no!" protested Zillah. "You can't think of giving that baby to Damaris."

"We can keep her," suggested Don, who had apparently experienced a change of heart now that Rose was clean. "I'll let her have my bed."

"No, dears," Marcia said slowly. "We must let Damaris decide if she wants to keep the child. Damaris is her family."

"Mr. Rose was her family, too, and he didn't want her," Cyril pointed out. "Maybe there's somethin' wrong with her. Joe Roe had a pup he couldn't keep, on account of it had fleas so bad."

"Mandy Rose does not have fleas!" Zillah said.

"We'll wait and see," said Stuart, and everyone turned to look at him. "About whether Damaris wants to keep the baby, I mean," he said. "Not about the fleas." Marcia wrote a note to Damaris Drybread and sent Rupert to carry it. Then the family settled down to prepare supper.

Ru returned just as the table was set. "She said she'll be coming for Mandy," he said, shaking his head, "but she didn't look happy."

"She *never* looks happy," Adah reminded him.

"Children!" Marcia reprimanded them, though her voice was soft. "Show some charity. Damaris's sister has just died."

Mandy Rose was still with them when Reverend Lord came and knocked on the door. Marcia was explaining to him about the baby when Damaris finally arrived.

"You read the note?" Marcia asked her. "I am so sorry about your sister, Damaris. I will keep you in my prayers."

"I read it," Damaris sniffed, "and I had to think about whether to come get the child or not."

Had to think about it! Millie bit her tongue. What kind of woman would have to think twice about taking in her own niece?

"But you Keiths certainly don't need another mouth to feed, and it would seem to be my Christian duty. Where is she?"

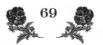

Marcia motioned to the cradle in the corner. "She is sleeping in Annis's cradle at the moment."

"She's smaller than I thought," Damaris observed, looking the baby over.

"I've put some nappies in a bag for you, Damaris," Marcia said. "And some of Annis's old things, enough to make do for a few days, and we are giving you a bucket of milk and, of course, the bottle. Why don't you sit with us and get to know each other?"

"Yes, do, Miss Drybread," Reverend Lord urged. "Perhaps you would like to sit by the stove and get warm while we read?" He held up *The Sketch Book of Geoffrey Crayon, Gent.* "We will be reading a great story from this collection of short stories—*Rip Van Winkle* by Mr. Washington Irving."

"Reverend, I am surprised at you!" Damaris said.

"Really?" Reverend Lord took a step back.

"Is that, or is it not, a novel?"

"No," Reverend Lord said. "Yes. Well . . . not really. It's a compilation of short stories."

"But it is *fiction*." The corners of Damaris's mouth were turned down. "My father always said that the reading of fiction by young women agitates their fancies and opens to their view elysian fields that exist only in the imagination. It will end in sorrow and wretchedness."

"What's that mean?" Cyril asked.

"It means she thinks it will give them an unrealistic view of the world," Marcia translated.

"Well, of course it's not real," Ru said. "It's made up."

"Children!" Stuart's voice was firm. "We beg your pardon, Miss Drybread. They are used to speaking their minds. Sit with us for a time, and we will discuss other things."

"I think not," Damaris said. "I'll take the child and go." She gathered Mandy Rose in her arms in a rather stiff and awkward manner and headed for the door. The baby, held against Damaris's shoulder, reached her little arms out to Millie as she went past and started to cry.

"None of that," Damaris said, looking at Mandy Rose sternly.

Stuart opened the door for Damaris and helped her down the steps and up into her sleigh wagon. She settled the baby beside her on the seat, lifted and snapped the reins, and the old horse plodded forward, pulling the wagon slowly through the snow.

"Bye, baby," Fan said, her little nose pressed against the windowpane.

How horrible! Millie kept the thought to herself, for Adah and Zillah were already weeping for the baby.

"Aunty," Millie asked after the children had gone to bed and Reverend Lord started his cold walk home, "were your walks in Lansdale ever so exciting?"

"Goodness, yes," Aunt Wealthy replied. "Walks always are. They are a bit like travel, don't you think? You never know what will happen next. I remember the time I trod on the toe of a count. He was in this country for his health, you see, and the air was supposed to strengthen his lungs. I quite squashed his foot, I'm afraid, and he used the name of the Lord in vain. That led to a conversation."

Millie smiled. She could just imagine how that conversation started, and how surprised the count must have been. "It turned out that it was a divine appointment. The poor man had never really understood who Jesus was. At any rate," Aunt Wealthy continued, "he accepted the Lord. And that night he succumbed to his lung ailment, quite sud-

denly. I saw his name in the paper the next day. It was too bad, really. He was a dashing young man. And he came all the way from Germany, just so I could step on his toe and tell him about Jesus."

Millie took her time brushing her hair before the mirror that night. If God cared enough about a dashing German count to send him all the way to Lansdale, Ohio, surely He cared about Mandy Rose. *Lord,* Millie prayed, *I know Aunt Wealthy says that sometimes we don't understand. But could You please help me understand why You would send such a sweet baby to that woman?*

The next time the Keiths saw Mandy Rose was at church, and the child was wearing one of Annis's old smocks. Damaris had pulled out every decorative stitch and snipped off the tiny bows that had once decorated the bib. Millie felt her face grow hot, remembering all the hours of work Mamma had put into the adornments for Annis.

If Marcia noticed that they were missing, however, she didn't mention it. "She is looking so much better, Damaris," she said. "Look at those rosy cheeks." Mandy smiled and reached for her. "You must be doing something right."

Millie was sure the corners of the teacher's mouth softened, possibly almost turned up, but Damaris turned away abruptly, and when she turned back, her stern schoolmarm face was firmly in place. "She seems to be a reasonable child," she admitted, setting Mandy Rose on a blanket under the pew. In Millie's opinion, the baby was more than reasonable. She interrupted the sermon only once or twice with gurgles. When members of the congregation commented on how well

Mandy Rose had behaved, Damaris frowned. "I would prefer you not compliment the child while it is present," she said. "I don't want it spoiled."

Mandy Rose looked up at Damaris and held up her arms.

In time, the Keiths' home had become a gathering place for the young people of Pleasant Plains. Wallace Ormsby, Nicholas Ransquate, Rhoda Jane, and Gordon—everyone was assured of a welcome at the Keiths' table with lively conversation. Claudina was a frequent guest, as was Gordon. They caused something of a diversion for the children by blushing and stuttering when they spoke to each other. Rhoda Jane visited several times a week, and she often dropped by with Gordon and the others on Sunday afternoons. Gordon was involved in every conversation, and particularly liked to listen when Stuart or Reverend Lord were discussing the Bible or church services. It was only when Claudina joined the group that he appeared to be tongue-tied. In fact, the very first Sunday after sitting in the Keiths' kitchen and speaking with Stuart, Gordon showed up at church. He sat in the back pew, and Millie was not quite sure whether he was staring at Reverend Lord or the back of Claudina's bonnet. But no matter which it was, at least he was hearing the sermon, because he discussed it quite intelligently that afternoon.

One Sunday in late February, Reverend Lord was invited to join the Keiths for dinner at their home after the service.

"You haven't forgotten that we were going to dine together, Reverend Lord?" Nicholas Ransquate asked, joining the group.

"No, of course not," Reverend Lord said, flushing. He turned to Marcia. "I am afraid I have a previous engagement, Mrs. Keith. I try to meet with each of the young men of my church once a month, and I have already invited Mr. Ransquate to dine with me."

"Why don't you bring him as your guest?" Marcia suggested. "I am sure there will be plenty of food, and you can have a private discussion as you walk home." Nicholas readily agreed to the plan, and the whole party started out together, walking the short distance to the Big Yellow House. Water ran beneath the snow on each side of the path, tinkling like tiny bells. The leaf buds on trees and bushes were swollen with the promise of spring. Winter was releasing its hold on Pleasant Plains at last. Millie and Claudina brought up the rear, walking arm in arm and enjoying the soft early-spring air. Just ahead of them walked Aunt Wealthy and Reverend Lord, then Wallace, Nicholas, and Celestia Ann, with Stuart and Marcia in front. The young Keiths ran ahead, bursting with energy after their long sit in church.

"Celestia Ann certainly has improved by her association with the Keiths," Claudina remarked.

Millie watched Nicholas take Celestia Ann's elbow as she stepped daintily over a slushy patch in the trail. She looked nothing at all like the seventeen-year-old tomboy who had arrived on their doorstep the year before looking for work. Her red hair had then been a bird's nest of tangles, and she had worn men's overalls beneath her faded gingham dress. Celestia Ann had always loved Jesus; her mischievous, merry heart was the same as it had been on that first day. But now the young woman ahead of them was the picture of a lady, her auburn curls pulled back from her pixie face.

"We haven't changed her a bit," Millie said. "She has decided to improve herself."

"Well, I'm not the only one who has noticed," Claudina giggled. Millie knew that was true. Several of the young men at church went out of their way to sit by the Keiths' housekeeper. She treated them all with friendly smiles, just as if they were her brothers. "Bill went to Nicholas's shop for new boots last week," Claudina continued, "and he said Nicholas could talk of nothing else. Nicholas said he's going to marry Celestia Ann!"

Reverend Lord, walking just ahead of them, stopped so suddenly that Claudina ran into him with some force. Reverend Lord was a tall young man, but Claudina was a sturdy girl, and that combined with the icy condition of the path and the fact that Wannago chose that instant to dart under his feet sent him staggering off the path. He sank to his knees in the wet, slushy snow.

"Oh! I'm so sorry!" Claudina said, clapping her hand over her mouth.

"Oh, dear," Aunt Wealthy said, snapping her umbrella closed and offering the handle to assist the preacher with his predicament.

The rest of the group heard the commotion and turned in time to see Reverend Lord attempting to pull his feet from the slush, which he managed at the expense of one shoe. He hopped about on one foot for a moment until Aunt Wealthy steadied him, then he leaned over and managed to retrieve the shoe, now full of mud.

"Are you all right?" Nicholas asked.

"Quite all right," Reverend Lord said, standing on one foot. "Quite all right."

"I don't think you can put that on," Aunt Wealthy said, indicating the shoe.

"I'm afraid you're right." He poured out a pool of water, but the shoe was still full of mud.

"I'll carry you piggyback," Nicholas offered. "It's not far, and I am very strong." He smiled at Celestia Ann.

"No, thank you," Reverend Lord said, flushing. "I'll . . . hop."

"Hop?" Nicholas responded, looking amused.

"Yes," Reverend Lord said with determination. "As you said, it's not far. Shall we go?"

The group continued, Reverend Lord looking like a one-legged crow — his elbows wide for balance, the tails of his Sunday suit flapping each time he hopped.

"You seemed a bit . . . distracted during your sermon today, Reverend Lord, although you made some excellent points," Aunt Wealthy said when he paused to rest. "Is everything well with you?"

"To tell you the truth, Miss Stanhope, I haven't been sleeping well," Reverend Lord confessed. "There is much on my mind." The whole group had stopped to wait for him to catch his breath, and he flushed again when he noticed this.

"Look! Pussy willows!" Zillah exclaimed, pointing to the cluster of tall, skinny stalks by the side of the road.

"I love pussy willows!" Celestia Ann said. Nicholas produced a pocketknife, leapt artfully to an exposed log, then from rock to rock until he reached the pussy willows. He returned with an armful and presented them to Celestia Ann.

"Thank you kindly," she said excitedly. "The first bouquet of spring!"

Nicholas attempted one of his stiff bows, but it was cut short by a slushy snowball smacking his back. Adah and Zillah giggled.

"Cyril!" Stuart admonished.

"Don't reprimand him too severely, sir," Nicholas said, brushing the slush from his shoulder. "Boys will be boys! I've done the same myself." But Millie didn't like the look he gave Cyril when Stuart turned away.

At dinner, pussy willows in a vase presided over the excellent meal prepared by Celestia Ann and Aunt Wealthy. Aunt Wealthy had cleaned Reverend Lord's shoe for him, and with the exception of the mud on his pants he was as good as new. The conversation turned to the sermon, which had been on the topic of forgiveness.

"Surely you can't mean that Jesus would have us be cowardly?" Nicholas inquired.

"No," Reverend Lord replied. "It seems to me that it takes more courage not to strike back, especially if one is strong. Think of what courage Jesus had, to take a beating and to be crucified, when at any moment He could have ended it all with a word. The point was, the stronger had mercy on the weaker. He had nothing but love in His heart. And sometimes it takes courage to love."

The discussion went on, sometimes quite vigorously, but Millie's mind went back to the Christmas Eve service, and the expression on her mother's face when she was speaking to Damaris. The stronger had mercy on the weaker. *I don't think I can do that,* Millie admitted silently to the Lord. *Damaris Drybread is the one person on earth I don't think I can ever love!*

Celestia Ann had outdone herself with the meal, making sure there were two desserts from which to choose on this

occasion. Nicholas had a piece of each, and complimented both. Reverend Lord didn't seem to have an appetite and, in fact, looked pale and out of sorts.

"Won't you have a piece of pie?" Millie asked him. "It really is excellent."

"No, no thank you," Reverend Lord said. "In fact, I think it's time we were going." He stood and waited for Nicholas who, after a moment's hesitation, rose also. The two young men left together, shaking Stuart's hand and thanking Marcia for her hospitality, and the Keith home settled down for a quiet Sunday afternoon. While Claudina and Millie were helping Celestia Ann clear the table, there came a knock at the door. Millie answered it to find Reverend Lord standing on the step in a clean, mudless suit.

"I fear I . . . forgot my book," he said.

"Won't you come in?" Millie stepped aside. She looked down the street but Nicholas Ransquate was nowhere in sight. Reverend Lord followed her to the kitchen and took up his customary chair by the stove. Sunday afternoons were a day of rest for the Keiths. Celestia Ann did not cook supper on this day, as there were plenty of leftovers from dinner to eat. Reverend Lord was apparently not planning on leaving, although he was uncharacteristically quiet. When it was time for supper, Millie set a place for him at the table.

After their light meal, Stuart turned to Reverend Lord. "It is quite possible that we are blessed to have both the greatest preacher and the finest cook in all of Indiana in our home today."

"I agree about the preaching, Mr. Keith!" Celestia Ann said, smiling.

"And what do you think, Reverend Lord?" Aunt Wealthy asked.

"I share your high opinion of the cook, but can hardly say the same for the preaching. This apple pie, for instance, would never put Mr. Monocker to sleep!"

"You underestimate yourself," Aunt Wealthy assured him. "Your sermons are becoming more thought-provoking every week. You are challenging your flock!"

Several voices at the table agreed, but when the comments died down the room seemed unnaturally quiet. Reverend Lord was staring at his napkin.

Fan asked suddenly, "Can preachers get married?"

Marcia's face grew red with embarrassment. "Why, Fan, of course they can. But, precious one, let's talk of something else, shall we?" she said quickly to the little girl.

"But why, Mamma?" Fan asked, her eyes wide. "Why doesn't Reverend Lord have his *own* wife to cook for him?"

All eyes shifted to Reverend Lord and the color drained from his face.

Reverend Lord rose from his chair, lifted his eyes to heaven as if to give him courage, then started around the table. "I lift up my eyes . . . where does my help come from? My help comes from You, my Lord and the Maker of heaven and earth . . ." he whispered to himself.

Was Millie imagining it because of his ghostly white face, or was Reverend Lord praying under his breath as he passed her chair? He walked around the table and sank to one knee beside Celestia Ann's chair. "Miss Huntsinger," he said, his deep voice shaking. "Will you . . . will you . . ."

Millie thought for one horrible moment that he would lose his courage and flee, but Celestia Ann looked into his eyes. "Will I . . . make apple pies for the next potluck? Yes, I will!"

"You will!" He looked as if he had been handed the world, then blinked. "Apple pies? What I meant was will you . . .?" Once again the words seemed to stick in his throat.

"Try an occasional peach cobbler?" She looked demurely at her lap. "Yes!"

Desperation was settling visibly over the good reverend.

"Don't stop now, Reverend! You've gotten two yesses! You're on a roll!" Aunt Wealthy cried.

Stuart rose and laid a hand on Reverend Lord's shoulder. "Courage, Lord," he said. "Give him courage."

Reverend Lord took a deep breath. He looked up into Celestia Ann's eyes and suddenly blurted out, "Willyoubemy wife?"

"Yes, I will!" Celestia Ann exclaimed.

"You will? You will!" He leapt to his feet. "She said yes! She's going to marry me!" he announced to everyone at the table.

"Yes, we heard," said Aunt Wealthy, sitting back in her chair, mopping her brow with her napkin, and sighing. "That was the most romantic thing I have ever seen!"

"Married! Why . . . they can't get married," Cyril shouted, standing up so quickly that he knocked over his chair.

"Why, Cyril!" Marcia exclaimed. "What has come over you? Why can't they get married?"

"Because!" Cyril said angrily, his face flushing with embarrassment. " 'Cause you . . . you have to kiss to get married!" he said, pointing an accusing finger at Reverend Lord. "And . . . and preachers can't kiss!" Cyril stammered. The room erupted into laughter, and Cyril fled for the stairs.

Marcia started to follow him, but Stuart took her hand. Leaning over to speak into her ear, he said quietly, "Let him

have a few moments alone. A broken heart is a very serious thing for a young boy. I will talk with him later."

"Isn't romance wonderful?" Claudina asked, watching the figures of Reverend Lord and Celestia Ann as they walked together. Aunt Wealthy had shooed them outside where they could have some privacy, and Stuart had collared Cyril and Don as they tried to escape out the back door and follow the couple.

Millie gazed out the window. Celestia Ann was holding on to Reverend Lord's arm, and his head was bent toward her, listening to what she had to say. "I am glad that Reverend Lord and Celestia Ann are in love," Millie said. "They seem so perfect for each other that I'm sure that God had their romance secretly planned in His heart, just waiting to surprise them with it."

"How do you think they knew they were in love?" Claudina rubbed a smudge from the windowpane with her fingertip. "I mean, knew for certain?"

"I haven't thought of it much," Millie said. "Mrs. Lightcap and Rhoda Jane had their suspicions, but it seems to me that Celestia Ann and Reverend Lord kept their secret in their hearts, speaking to no one but God about it."

Claudina covered her face with her hands. "I fear I am not so adept at keeping my heart a secret. I can almost keep from blushing when Gordon speaks to me, but if he smiles, I am lost!"

Lord, what do I say? Can this be right? Millie took Claudina's hands in her own. "You can't mean that you are in love with Gordon Lightcap?" she said. "You are only fourteen!"

"And Gordon is seventeen. Some people marry when they are not much older. You can't tell me you never think of any young man, Millie."

"Well," Millie said, "truthfully, I do wonder sometimes if God has a young man for me. Perhaps he wants me to be single all my life, like Aunt Wealthy. She seems happy enough. The more I taste of adventure, the more I like it. You have no idea how exciting a simple prayer walk can be."

"I will never be happy until I am married," Claudina sighed. "And I am sure my heart is going to break. Father will never approve of Gordon. He has no prospects."

"Is wealth that important?" Millie asked.

"Of course," Claudina said. "If I married Gordon, I would have to cook and clean and do endless work. I might even have to labor like Mrs. Lightcap, taking in other people's laundry. Father would never allow such a thing. You can't tell me your father would allow *you* to marry Gordon."

"I have no desire to marry anyone," Millie said.

"But if you did? Would your father allow it?"

"No," Millie said slowly. "I'm sure he would not. But not because of wealth or social standing. Pappa would ask first if Gordon was a Christian."

"But he is a good man. And if you were in love with him, surely that wouldn't matter so much. You would be with him day and night, showing him how a Christian behaves. He could become a Christian after you were married. You have to be sensible about these things."

"I think it would be sensible if you waited a few years for romance," Millie said.

"My heart is not sensible, then," Claudina sighed.

CHAPTER 7

Sealed with a Kiss

As a bridegroom rejoices over his bride, so will your God rejoice over you.

ISAIAH 62:5

The wedding of Reverend Lord and Celestia Ann was set for early May. Marcia and Aunt Wealthy started sewing the bride's trousseau. The young couple was turning Reverend Lord's small home into a honeymoon cottage, and if the Keiths' new house was finished on schedule, it would serve as the reception hall.

Meanwhile, the stagecoach road to Pleasant Plains was pushed through in early April. The first conveyances to travel on it were wagons loaded with lumber for the new stable. Ru was fascinated by the work, and he listened avidly to the workmen describing the building of the road; he later repeated all the details at the dinner table.

The ground was still wet and marshy with spring runoff, and each rain tore away soil from the newly exposed land where the workmen had cut trees and cleared bushes. The wagon drivers were sometimes forced to recreate the road where it had dissolved into marsh or completely washed away. This they accomplished by laying logs and saplings side by side to form a solid surface. The solution was only temporary, for though it kept the heavy wagons from sinking to the hub in the soft mud, the gaps between the logs were a hazard to horses, and there were several leg injuries. Road crews followed behind, making diversion channels here and building up the road with gravel there.

Gordon cleared and leveled the site of the stable, working alone from before sunup until the last light faded on every day but Sunday. Stuart and Reverend Lord organized the men of the church for a stable-raising, and Marcia and Celestia Ann took the ladies in hand, arranging a potluck dinner and a dance.

The men arrived at the Lightcaps' early on the appointed day, bringing their own hammers and saws. Stuart divided them into teams and gave each team its assignments. Much to Ru's delight, he was drafted to work alongside the men. Cyril and Don were kept busy carrying buckets of nails.

Millie divided her time between cooking for the party and carrying water to the workers. The stable rose almost like magic—the stacks of lumber transforming into a building almost before her eyes. By noon the framing was done and the walls were being closed in.

Around dinnertime the ladies began to arrive by foot, by horse, and by wagon, carrying baskets of food. Sawhorses and boards were made into banquet tables and piled high with every kind of food. The men worked faster as the smell of fried chicken and fresh bread drifted on the breeze.

At last everything but the finish work—the hanging of doors and framing of windows—was done. Millie, Claudina, and Rhoda Jane walked through the stable with Gordon, inspecting each wall and beam.

Gordon ran his hand along the wall between two stalls. "I don't have the words . . ." His voice trailed off as he stared in amazement.

"Beyond belief!" Rhoda Jane offered, laughing. "Inconceivable, unimaginable, impossible. Simply put, too good to be true! You need to read more, brother of mine."

"That's it exactly!" Gordon said. "Too good to be true. But it didn't happen because of books, sister. Men built it with the strength of their backs and the skill in their hands."

But it did happen because of a Book, Millie wanted to say. *Because Pappa believes the Bible when it commands us to love our*

neighbors as ourselves. Because Pappa is a doer of the Word and not a hearer only. God is changing the lives of the Lightcap family, changing all of Pleasant Plains. Can't Gordon and Rhoda Jane see it? Can't they see God's mighty fingerprints in everything that is happening to them?

"Ladies will stay in the front yard, please," Marcia called when they came out of the stable.

A washtub had been filled with hot water and set behind the newly constructed walls of the stable. A line of work-weary men holding packages containing fresh shirts and pants disappeared around one corner, and one by one they reappeared from behind the other corner, washed and ready for the dinner and dance. One or two had added a splash of rose water when they combed their hair, and the clean scent drifted about in the warm summer air.

Gordon took his place in line, then changed his mind and walked over to where Rhoda Jane, Millie, and Claudina were talking. He stopped beside them, gazing up at the building again, fingers locked and hands on top of his head.

"I thought you were going to clean up," Rhoda Jane said.

"I can't stand still long enough to wait in line," Gordon said, smiling and bouncing on his toes like a young child. "I'll go last."

"The water will be cold and dark as mud," Rhoda Jane warned. Gordon simply shrugged, chuckling softly to himself and shaking his head as he continued to stare up at the building.

Stuart approached the group just as Rhoda Jane was warning Gordon to get in line to wash himself. "What is it, Gordon?" Stuart asked, coming to stand beside him and

look up in the direction of Gordon's gaze. Millie and Claudina turned to hear Gordon's answer.

"I'm thinking," Gordon said seriously, "that little things make a big difference. Like nails that turn lumber into a building. Nails and know-how, that's what did it. The wood is solid. You see the wood, but it's the nails that make it work."

"I never thought of it that way before." Stuart gave Gordon a quizzical look. "But you are right. It's hard to build without nails. When God decided to build a church, he started with nails in a Carpenter's hands."

"Come on, Gordy," Rhoda Jane said, taking his arm and pulling him away suddenly. "No one's going to want to dance with you if you don't get cleaned up." Stuart shook his head as he watched them go.

Millie and Claudina went to help Aunt Wealthy with the tables. She had set the smaller children to work with fans, shooing flies away from the tables heavy with food.

"Where is Mrs. Lightcap?" Reverend Lord asked. "She should be here for the blessing of the food."

"She said she was going for a walk," Zillah said, pointing. "Up the hill."

"I'll find her." Millie was glad to get away by herself for a while, climbing up above the festivities. *Is Rhoda Jane's heart ever going to soften, Lord? Is she ever going to want to know more about You? It's bad enough that she won't listen, but she won't let Gordon listen either. It breaks my heart. It must break Yours, too. Help me be the kind of friend who will never give up on her.*

Millie was shaken from her thoughts as she looked up and saw Mrs. Lightcap sitting on a log halfway up the hill, gazing down at the stable. "Mrs. Lightcap?" Millie called to her. "Are you all right?"

"Yes," said Mrs. Lightcap. She waved her arm at the stable below. "You know, I didn't believe it was going to be real, not until this afternoon when I saw it standing before me. I'd thought, 'At least the idea of it has given my children hope, even if it never happens.' But look at it now — as solid and real as anything! Your father is the one who did it, you know. He is the one who made this dream come true."

"Pappa would say it was God who made it happen," Millie said. "God expects us to help one another."

Mrs. Lightcap smiled. "Is that what he would say? Well, I will say my thanks to the Keiths. If there is a God, and if He cares, maybe He will hear that."

She sounds just like Rhoda Jane. I wish I could be clever and say the right thing, like Pappa always does. Millie waited, but nothing witty, clever, or wise came to mind.

"Everyone is waiting for you," Millie said at last, offering her hand. Mrs. Lightcap took it and stood up. They walked together down the hill.

The food was blessed, and for a time there was laughter and conversation while people filled their plates. As the twilight settled over the festivities, the lanterns were lit. Mr. Roe produced his fiddle, and the dancing began.

Millie found her father sprawled on a chair on the porch of the stable. His long legs were stretched out before him and his arms hung at his sides, but he had a contented look on his sunburnt face. Millie sat down on the step at his feet. Claudina was dancing with Gordon, who had apparently taken Rhoda Jane's advice, and possibly some of Nicholas Ransquate's rose water. Mrs. Chetwood stood watching them, her lips pursed. Rhoda Jane herself sat on a corral rail with York, laughing and sipping the punch he had brought her. Reverend Lord danced awkwardly with

Celestia Ann, but both of them were laughing and she seemed to be able to keep her toes out from under his feet.

"Pappa? How do you know when you are in love?" Millie asked.

Stuart sat suddenly upright. "Are you inquiring on your own behalf, or that of another?"

"Don't worry," Millie laughed. "I don't fancy myself in love with anyone. I just wondered how you *know*."

"That is a relief," Stuart said, slumping into his chair again. "That is a very serious question, daughter, and not one I had anticipated hearing for a few more years. I'm not sure I can answer it without a great deal of thought."

"How much thought?" Millie asked.

"Six or seven years should be enough time for me to think it through properly and weigh my words carefully."

"Pappa!"

"All right, then. At least let me sleep on it and I will pray desperately for wisdom."

"I thought you always knew what to say," Millie teased.

"You are much too precious to me and that is much too serious a question for me to take it lightly," Stuart said.

Marcia had left the serving table and she now made her way to the porch. "Hello, dearest," she said, bending to kiss the top of her husband's head.

"Ouch," Stuart said.

"Ouch?" Marcia laughed. "I barely touched you. It was a butterfly kiss!"

"I know it," Stuart said. "But there is no part of my body that does not hurt. Remind me of this, Marcia. I am a lawyer, not a carpenter. I am an old lawyer, far too old to build stables all day long. Look at this." He held up his hands. "Blisters! I won't be able to write for a week."

"Poor dear," Marcia said, taking his hands. "I am proud of my old lawyer. Do you suppose I could convince him to dance with me?"

"Maybe," Stuart said.

"Maybe?"

"If you don't touch me anywhere."

"Come along." Marcia pulled him to his feet.

"Ouch! You're touching me!" Stuart said as she dragged him onto the dance floor.

Mrs. Lightcap is right, Millie decided. *My Pappa is a great man.*

"Now, about knowing when you're in love," Stuart said the next night as he sat on the edge of Millie's bed. "I did pray for wisdom, and I can tell you a little bit. But I reserve the right to amend—no, to add to—my case as you grow older."

He took Millie's Bible from the stand by her bed. "Being in love, the kind of love that will last a lifetime, starts right here, in 1 Corinthians 13:4. 'Love is patient, love is kind. It does not envy, it does not boast, it is not proud. It is not rude, it is not self-seeking, it is not easily angered, it keeps no record of wrongs. Love does not delight in evil but rejoices with the truth. It always protects, always trusts, always hopes, always perseveres. Love never fails.' If your feelings and your actions cannot stand up to these verses, then how could you be in love?"

"But Pappa, surely those verses are for all Christians. Isn't Paul saying that we should love everyone that way?"

"Yes, he is," Stuart laughed. "Practice it with all your might. You can start out practicing on your friends and

family, but if you really want to see what God can do, practice on your enemies. It takes a lot of work—and courage, too. But keep at it. And when it is time for you to fall in love, God will add something special and wonderful. Now, is that enough of an answer for tonight?"

"It's enough," Millie yawned. "For tonight. I expect I will have more questions later."

"I expect you will. I will try to grow wise before you do. And if I have not grown wise enough to have more answers, I will tell you to ask your mother. Goodnight, Millie dear."

Millie lay in the darkness for a moment after Pappa had left. *Love is patient. I know I am more patient than I was last year—especially with the little boys. But sometimes I could be more kind. I could do better in both of those areas.* Millie threw off her covers and lit the candle at her writing table. She lay a clean sheet of paper beside her Bible and copied the verse carefully word for word. She blotted the ink, and waved the paper in the air until it was dry. Then she turned it over. Millie started her list with Pappa, and put a tiny heart by his name. Then Mamma and Aunt Wealthy and Ru and the other children. After she wrote Annis in at the bottom of the family tree, she included Rhoda Jane and the Lightcaps; Claudina and Helen and Lu; Matthew Lord and Celestia Ann. She prayed for each one as she wrote the name. When the ink was dry, she tucked the list into her Bible, climbed back into bed, and pulled the cover up to her nose.

Help me learn to love them the way You do, Jesus, she prayed. *Remind me to practice every day!*

When the stagecoach rolled into Pleasant Plains on the second day of May, 1834, the stable was finished and the Lightcaps were ready. After the townsfolk insisted, Gordon hung a sign over the entrance to the building. Now, hand-carved in bas-relief, a stagecoach and four horses raced across a wooden sign that read, "Lightcap's Livery Stable."

The entire town turned out for the occasion, ladies in their most stylish bonnets and men in their Sunday best. Mr. Grange, who would be the first passenger to ride the stagecoach out of Pleasant Plains, tried to give a speech, but no one could be convinced to listen. Millie was busy searching the crowd for Cyril, who had disappeared. She had enlisted the help of Adah, Zillah, and Emmaretta in her search, but they had given up after looking in the hayloft and empty rain barrels, and were sitting in the bed of the Roes' wagon, scanning the crowd.

"Look, Millie." Zillah tugged on Millie's apron string and pointed. "There's Mandy Rose." Damaris Drybread, who was making her way through the crowd toward a group of mothers with young children, had Mandy Rose balanced on her hip. No one could deny that the baby was blooming, even under Damaris's strict care. She was a sweet and loving child, quick to give baby kisses and smiles. She had a positive genius for being adorable. She loved attention.

When Mandy Rose had decided to take her first steps, she wasn't satisfied to do so in the privacy of the Drybread home. She pulled herself up on the church pew during Reverend Lord's sermon and took her first tottering steps toward the preacher. The whole congregation caught its breath, and Mandy Rose looked at everyone and clapped her hands in delight. But the more lovable Mandy Rose became, the more

the other women disapproved of Damaris's strict rules about candy, naps, and plain clothing.

"That little one is pure gold," Mrs. Roe would often say. "It wouldn't hurt to let her have a frill or a bit of lace."

"How can Miss Drybread have such a wonderful baby?" Zillah asked one day.

Marcia looked across the room at Damaris, who was holding Mandy Rose on her lap. "Babies don't need candy, or ribbons and bows," Marcia said. "Babies need love."

"You mean Miss Drybread *loves* her? How can you tell?" Ru asked curiously.

"I just can," Marcia said. Millie had been watching Damaris ever since, trying to see a little glimmer of what Marcia saw in Damaris Drybread.

Damaris bounced Mandy Rose higher on her hip as she reached the group of laughing women, but just as she was about to speak they turned their backs on her. She turned away, as if she hadn't intended to join them at all, but Millie saw her arms tighten around Mandy Rose.

"I wouldn't talk to her, either," Zillah said. "All she talks about is how angry God is."

Suddenly a sharp sound rent the air. "It's a bugle!" someone cried. "The stagecoach is coming!"

The bugle called again and then they saw it. The driver had whipped the team to a run, just to make a show of his arrival. There was a small figure sitting beside him, and as Millie watched, it stood and put the bugle to its lips.

"Cyril!" Marcia yelled. "Sit down right now!" Cyril was clearly too far away to hear. He held onto the driver's shoulder with one hand, lifted the bugle with the other, and blew with all his might. The stagecoach thundered towards them. At the last moment, the coachman grabbed the brake

lever and gave a mighty pull, at the same time drawing back on the reins. The horses reared as the coach lurched to a stop, making a show indeed.

Cyril bowed to the audience.

"Cyril Keith! I said sit down."

"Aw, Mamma!" Cyril protested. "I ain't gonna fall. We're not even movin'."

"This one yours, ma'am?" The driver caught Cyril by the suspenders and swung him out over thin air. "He jumped onto the stage outta a tree a few miles down the road, and it's a good thing he held on. Could have broke his fool neck. If I'd had any passengers, he'd have plumb scared them to death."

"Hey!" Cyril said, kicking his feet. "Let me go!"

"I'll take that parcel," Stuart said, and the driver dropped Cyril into his arms.

"I'll need my bugle back, boy." The driver spat a stream of tobacco juice, and several ladies moved back, pulling their skirts out of the way. Cyril handed the bugle up to him, and Stuart set Cyril on the ground. He promptly wiggled his way through the crowd to where Don and Fan were standing near Millie.

"Some brother you are," Don said, giving him a shove. "Runnin' off without me."

"You'd have told," Cyril said. "You always tell."

Don glanced toward his pappa. "Only if it's wrong."

"Ay-yup," Cyril said, trying to spit as the driver had and failing. "That's what I mean." He wiped the drizzle from his chin.

"Gentlemen do not spit, Cyril Keith," said Millie. "And if you want to stay and watch, I suggest you mind your manners."

"Got some mail!" the driver called, opening the boot and producing two letters. "Both for Damaris Drybread."

Damaris made her way to the front of the crowd. "Thank you. And could you take these?" She handed him a small stack of letters in return. People stared, clearly wondering who would be writing to Damaris, and who she would be writing to, but Damaris just put her nose in the air, hoisted Mandy Rose higher on her hip, and made her way out of the crowd.

"And these here," the driver said, lifting out a stack of newspapers bound together with twine, "are for a Mr. Stuart Keith."

"Ahhhhhhh," Stuart said, taking his papers. "Smell that ink! Fresh off the presses."

"Anything else?" Bill Chetwood asked hopefully.

"Nope," the driver said, and he spat again. "That's it."

"How 'bout news?" asked Mrs. Roe, who was always eager for gossip.

"Not much." The driver climbed down from his perch and hitched up his pants. "Crick rose in Lambertville and washed away two cabins. Fellow in Hansen killed him a hydrophoby skunk, but not before it bit his wife. She went crazy, poor critter, and will probably have passed by the time I get back that way. You folks might be on the lookout—that ain't mor'n fourteen miles from here. Where'm I s'posed to get grub?" As people began to drift away, back to their homes and work, Rhoda Jane brought the driver something to eat from the Lightcaps' house—which was serving as the way station's kitchen while the Keiths were still living in the warehouse.

Millie looked longingly after her father and his stack of newspapers, but decided it might be prudent to watch over

Don until the coach was gone. Don didn't like to be out-shone by his brother, and he had been eyeing the empty space in the boot. She leaned against the wall and watched as the boys helped Gordon with the team.

"What's hydrophoby?" Don asked, filling a nosebag with oats and handing it to Gordon.

"Hydrophobia," Gordon said. "It's a sickness that animals get." He slipped the bag over the horse's nose and settled the strap behind its ears. "Makes them act funny. Even shy little bunnies will attack humans if they have hydrophobia."

"I ain't afraid of bunnies," Cyril scoffed.

"I am," Gordon said quietly, "if they have hydrophobia, and you should be, too. If an animal with hydrophobia bites you, even a little bunny, you will die howling mad. There is no cure."

"How do you tell if animals are hydrophoby?" Zillah asked.

"They act crazy," Gordon said. "Aggressive. Towards the end, they stumble around and foam at the mouth."

Cyril bared his teeth and snarled at Emmaretta Lightcap like a vicious animal. "I'm a hydrophoby skunk," he growled. Emmaretta slugged him in the arm.

Reverend Matthew Lord was as poor as the proverbial churchmouse. The simple living he made came from tithes and gifts from the congregation, often in the form of eggs or bread rather than money. The money he did receive went, to a large extent, to supporting Piano's taste for corn. To her credit, she was growing fat and she had become a prolific milker. Reverend Lord had gallons more than he could drink, and he provided it free of charge to poor families. He had received at least two offers for the cow but as of yet had refused to sell. Piano followed him as faithfully as a dog, and if she escaped the pasture, he had only to whistle and she'd amble back.

One Sunday Mrs. Monocker asked him if he was ready to sell Piano after the cow had become lonely, leaned in the window, and mooed loudly during worship. Reverend Lord had flushed red, but Aunt Wealthy pointed out to Mrs. Monocker that Piano was *his* cow and he fed her from his own budget. "Besides," Aunt Wealthy added, "Piano is providing milk for God's children, and," she said, laying a kind hand on Reverend Lord's arm, "who else will listen so patiently as you practice your sermons? I think it is your kind attention that has fattened Piano, rather than the corn."

"I didn't think anyone knew about that," Reverend Lord said, turning even redder. "But she *is* a very good listener."

Reverend Lord's humble stone house had rooms that were stark and bachelor-like—one bedroom, a kitchen, and a sitting room that served double purpose as a library. He confessed one evening to the Keith family that his small house and his financial situation were what had kept him from speaking to Celestia Ann long ago. He had been concerned that no one could want such a husband.

"Have you starved yet, Matthew?" Celestia Ann asked.

"The Lord has always provided," Reverend Lord humbly replied.

"I expect He can feed two as easily as one," Celestia Ann had said. And that was that.

The people of Pleasant Plains, it seemed, had taken Reverend Lord into their hearts and they took it upon

themselves to see that he entered holy matrimony in proper style. Marcia and Aunt Wealthy, who had been sewing curtains for the Keiths' new home, used remnants to make curtains for Reverend Lord's house, and Aunt Wealthy contributed doilies and vases for the tabletops. Rhoda Jane threw a rug party, and the girls made a brightly-colored rug for the sitting room. Ru and Gordon and the young men built a white picket fence, and they made windowboxes for the front of the house, which Celestia Ann filled with wildflowers she transplanted from the prairie and marsh. Ru broke ground for a garden in the back, and Gordon put up a fence high enough to keep out the deer. When all was said and done, it was a perfect honeymoon cottage.

The Granges gave the grandest wedding gift of all for the pastor and his bride — the piano from their sitting room to be moved to the church. Mr. Tittlebaum pointed out that since there was a cow named Piano behind the church, they might as well call the piano Molly. Stuart's private opinion was that Mr. Tittlebaum might have been spending a little too much time with Aunt Wealthy.

The piano was given to the Lords well before the wedding, and it was installed temporarily in the sitting room of the Keiths' new house so it could be played during the ceremony. Afterwards, it would be moved to the church.

The night before the wedding, Millie found Celestia Ann arguing with Aunt Wealthy in the kitchen of the Keiths' new house.

"Don't be ridiculous," Aunt Wealthy said, waving a wooden spoon. "You can't bake your own wedding cake."

"Why not?" Celestia Ann inquired. "Matthew likes my cooking."

"It simply isn't done that way," Aunt Wealthy explained.

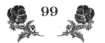

"I like to do things my own way," Celestia Ann responded. That was certainly true. Celestia Ann had sewn her own white wedding dress, refusing all offers of help and suggestions of style.

"How can you have time to prepare and bake a cake?" Aunt Wealthy asked in surprise. "Is your gown finished yet?"

Celestia Ann had to admit that it was not, and a compromise was reached. She baked the cake but left the decoration to Aunt Wealthy. The cake itself was not white, for the icing made from maple sugar was a light golden color, but Celestia Ann was determined that her household would follow the Keiths in their boycott of slave goods right from the start. Aunt Wealthy decorated the cake with roses crafted from icing, and even if it wasn't white, it was stunning. Cyril and Don were sternly admonished not to touch it, and Millie kept a close eye on them to make sure they obeyed.

On the morning of the wedding, Millie, Claudina, Rhoda Jane, Lu, and Helen gathered at the Keiths' house on the hill just after the sun came up. The sky was absolutely cloudless, promising a perfect day. The downstairs rooms of the house had been completed. Curtains and pictures were hung in every room and there were rugs on the floors.

The girls filled the rooms with vases of roses gathered from many gardens in town, and they set the reception table with Marcia's best silver. The workmen's full attention had been given to finishing the downstairs by the desired date, and no one would have guessed that the detailed woodwork of the sweeping stairs Celestia Ann was to walk down led up to an unfinished second story. When the girls had arranged and rearranged the flowers, Millie inspected each room, and she ended up in the kitchen for one last look at the cake. It showed evidence of

one small finger, but fortunately, none of the roses had been in the path of destruction, and Millie was able to smooth away the damage.

Celestia Ann arrived at nine o'clock, too nervous to even look at the roses. Aunt Wealthy whisked her to a small room at the top of the stairs where she put on her wedding gown, and the bride let Aunt Wealthy sweep her hair up into a glorious crown. Guests began arriving at ten, arranging themselves around the room in small groups.

"Millie," Marcia whispered, "keep an eye on Cyril for me. I confiscated his slingshot on the way over, but it would ease my mind if you stayed close to him." She need not have worried, though, because Stuart stationed himself behind Cyril.

The Reverend Arnold, a friend of Matthew Lord's who had agreed to perform the ceremony, arrived with Reverend Lord himself. Mrs. Grange, who had been sitting at the piano for at least forty-five minutes, began to play the moment Reverend Arnold was in place, holding his huge black Bible before him.

Reverend Lord's eyes lifted to the stairs as Celestia Ann appeared, and there was more than one murmur of approval. "I've never seen a more beautiful bride," Helen whispered. Claudina clasped her hands and seemed to hold her breath, exhaling only when Celestia Ann reached the last step.

Reverend Arnold performed a simple, sweet ceremony. Then, to Cyril's evident disgust, Reverend Lord proved that preachers can indeed kiss.

Aunt Wealthy was weeping quietly, as was Nicholas Ransquate, and Millie was surprised to see Damaris Drybread wipe a tear from her eye. Everyone wished the newlyweds well, and many prayers were offered for their bright future and long life together.

"What a perfect wedding," Claudina said, gazing across the room at Gordon Lightcap.

"Claudina?" Millie said. "Claudina!"

"Hmmmmmm?"

"Come with me." Millie dragged her friend out the door, past York Monocker who was smiling down at Rhoda Jane, past Mr. Tittlebaum who had cornered Aunt Wealthy again, off the porch and across the garden to the swing Ru had made for her. The sturdy wooden seat was wide enough for two. Millie forced Claudina to sit down, then she sat beside her.

"Pump your legs," Millie said. "I want to show you something." The swing was soon sailing high enough to see the ferryboat crossing the river and, in the other direction, the swamp. The whole world was spread before them, green and beautiful with summer. The view never failed to fill Millie's heart with longings for adventure and distant lands.

"Look!" Millie shouted as the swing paused at the top of its arc. "What do you see?" Swoosh! They came down, and then back up again.

"I see . . . I see . . . Gordon's house!" Claudina said.

Millie stopped pumping her legs, and the swing twisted crazily as it slowed down.

"Millie!" Claudina shrieked, clinging hard to the rope. "What on earth are you doing?"

"I was trying to get your mind off Gordon Lightcap."

"Oh." Claudina leaned her head against Millie's shoulder. "That's not going to happen. I'm in love!" Claudina giggled. "And don't tell me you have not noticed the way Wallace Ormsby is mooning over one Millie Keith," she said. "Love is just in the air these days."

8

A Dangerous Recipe

For I am the LORD, your God, who takes hold of your right hand and says to you, Do not fear; I will help you.

A Dangerous Recipe

S don't know what we would have done this last year without Celestia Ann," Marcia said as they walked back to the Big Yellow House after the wedding. "Or what we will do now, for that matter."

"God was very good to lend Celestia Ann to us for a season," Aunt Wealthy agreed. "That girl was a blessing from the first day she walked in the door."

"Fortunately, my girls are old enough to help their Mamma now," said Stuart.

"I'm big enough," Fan said, "but Annis is not. She's still a baby."

"Then it will be your job to watch Annis for your mother," Stuart said, pulling on Fan's pigtail.

What are we going to do without Celestia Ann, Lord? wondered Millie. In the year the Keiths had been in Pleasant Plains, a transformation had begun—they were truly becoming a frontier family. Millie's new life was a far cry from the life of privilege she had lived in Lansdale, with servants and shopkeepers ready to provide for her every need. But now she could do things she would never have imagined when she lived in Lansdale: milk a cow, make soap and candles, put up preserves. *I must admit that I do like to learn as much as I can learn, to grow as much as I can grow, and I love being friends with people from every kind of background — just like you were, Jesus.*

"Why so serious, my dear?" Aunt Wealthy asked, taking Millie's hand. "Didn't you think it was a delightful wedding?"

"Yes," Millie said, "it was wonderful. I was hoping that I can be as much of a help to Mamma as Celestia Ann was."

Aunt Wealthy squeezed her hand. "We will all have to do a little more, but I believe Philippians 4:13, that we can do everything through Christ Jesus who gives us strength," she said, sharing a familiar Bible verse.

The morning after Celestia Ann's wedding was washday, and Millie rose with the sun. Marcia and Aunt Wealthy were already up, heating water for the morning's wash. Ru had carried in bucket after bucket, enough to fill the big tub. The kitchen was full of stacks of laundry sorted into piles: white shirts and linens to be boiled, overalls and pants and workshirts to be washed in hot water and scrubbed clean on the washboard. Zillah and Adah came down the stairs behind Millie, rubbing the sleep out of their eyes.

"Good morning, sleepyheads," Aunt Wealthy said. "Who is going to help me this morning? I've found a marvelous recipe. I intend to fireproof the children."

"Fireproof the children?" Marcia poured a kettle of boiling water into the almost-full washtub. "Good heavens, Aunty!"

"It could save the life of a loved one. It says so right here," Aunt Wealthy said, waving her latest copy of *Lady's Book* magazine. "A Simple Recipe for Incombustible Clothing," she read. "One ounce of sal ammoniac added to the last water in which muslins or cottons are rinsed, and a similar quantity added to the starch with which they are stiffened, will render them practically un-inflammable. If they do burn, they will do so without flame. I have my sal ammoniac right here. If the experiment proves a success, then I will pass on the information at our next Ladies Society meeting. Can you imagine saving a life with a simple laundry technique?"

"I don't know, Aunty," Marcia said. "What if it ruins the fabric?"

"I plan to perform a test." Aunt Wealthy held up a dress that Annis had outgrown. "I will rinse this with the chemical, and add it to the starch as well. If the dress survives, I will treat all the children's clothing. Hand me my sal ammoniac, Zillah. It's on the table."

Aunt Wealthy measured a portion into the water, then dipped the dress in the mixture. She pulled it out and wrung it well. "There! Now I'll just speed up the drying a bit . . ." She opened the oven, laid the dress on the rack, and closed the door.

Millie moved Aunt Wealthy's concoctions aside to make room for her own project. She had decided to surprise the family by making Celestia Ann's special pancakes. Though she had never done the whole thing herself, the last time they were made she had watched Celestia Ann carefully, writing down each ingredient, measurement, and step. "Why are you doing that?" Celestia Ann had asked. "I just throw them together and they come out every time."

Millie set out her mixing bowls, spoons, flour, salt, and soda and took out her handwritten recipe. She measured and mixed the dry ingredients, then heated the skillet and laid thick slices of bacon on it to fry.

"I'm hungry," Cyril said as he entered the kitchen. "When's breakfast?"

"In just a few moments, I'm sure," Aunt Wealthy said, opening the oven and pulling out the dress. "Nice and dry!"

"We're eatin' dresses for breakfast?" Cyril scratched his head.

"We are having pancakes," Millie said. She cracked the eggs into a bowl and beat them into her milk. She finished measuring her dry ingredients, made a hole in the center, and poured in the egg-and-milk mixture. She beat it all with

the spoon until it was well-mixed, then she set a griddle on the stove top. When she poured a ladleful onto the griddle, it spread into a nice pool of dough, but it didn't rise and get bubbles the way Celestia Ann's always had. Millie frowned as she flipped it over. Every place it wasn't lumpy, it was rubbery and thin. A dozen batter puddles later, Millie had a stack of very flat pancakes. She went back over the recipe in her mind. She was sure she had measured correctly.

"I think they call those crepes in Belgium," Aunt Wealthy remarked. "Or is it France?"

"Never mind, Millie," Marcia said. "We are going to eat them up anyway."

Zillah set the table and called in the boys to wash their hands. Millie put a small stack of lumpcakes on each plate, along with a couple of strips of bacon.

"What is this?" Fan asked, poking the lumpy mass on her plate.

"It's a pancake," Millie replied, a bit downcast.

"You made these?" Don asked suspiciously. "By your ownself?"

Stuart, who had just entered the kitchen, looked at the table, then at Millie. "I'm sure they will *taste* wonderful," he said, "with a little maple syrup and some butter . . . Aunt Wealthy, whatever are you doing?"

Aunt Wealthy had opened the firebox on the cookstove with a mittened hand. The other hand held a poker, with Annis's dress suspended from the end like a festive flag.

"I have rendered this dress incombustible, Stuart," Aunt Wealthy said. "Watch!" She slid the dress into the firebox over the glowing coals. Cyril and Don crowded in to peer into the firebox, but Marcia shooed them away.

"One," Aunt Wealthy counted.

"It's smokin'," Don said, leaning around her.

"Two . . . three!" Aunt Wealthy said quickly, and she pulled out the dress. The edges were smoldering, and sparks glowed on the fabric itself. When it hit the rich air of the room, it burst into flame.

"Look out!" Cyril yelled. Zillah and Adah jumped back. Aunt Wealthy tried to shake out the flames, wielding the poker like a flaming sword, the dress clinging to the end. Finally, the fire burned through the dress and it fell to the floor. Aunt Wealthy lifted her skirts above her knees and stomped out the flames. "Well!" she said, straightening the bun at the top of her head. "Well! I simply must have done something wrong. The *Lady's Book* is a very reliable source. Very reliable."

"This wouldn't a 'happened if you hadn't let Celestia Ann get married," Cyril pointed out. Millie looked at the tins and bottles scattered across the tabletop.

"Zillah," she asked, "could you show me the sal ammoniac that you got for Aunty?" Zillah picked up the tin of baking soda and handed it to Millie.

"If Aunty has baking soda in her incombustible dress," Adah asked, "what has Millie got in her pancakes?"

Millie blushed. "I followed the recipe exactly," she said. "There is no sal ammoniac in my pancakes."

"*Those* came from Celestia Ann's recipe?" Ru asked, looking at the stack of lumpcakes. "Ah . . . I just remembered. Gordon asked me to come over early. He's shoeing Mr. Roe's mule, and I was going to help."

"Me, too," Cyril said.

"It's a big mule, Millie." Don edged toward the door. "Real mean, too. We'll get some apples at the stable. Apples are good for breakfast."

Millie's Courageous Days

"I miss Celestia Ann so much," Fan sighed as the boys escaped out the door.

"Now, Millie—" Marcia began, but Annis chose that moment to wake up and cry. "I'll be right back," Marcia said, hurrying up the stairs.

Millie started cleaning the mess from the tabletop, tears gathering in her eyes.

"Now don't let one little disaster dampen your spirits," said Stuart, as he scraped the remains of breakfast into the slop bucket. "I remember the first time your mother made her famous mashed potatoes."

"Could have used them for book paste," Aunt Wealthy said.

"We're out of book paste?" Marcia asked, carrying Annis into the room. "I thought I bought a whole pot full."

"Really?" Stuart said, winking at Aunt Wealthy behind her back. "Where did you put it?"

Aunt Wealthy performed her laundry experiment once again, this time using sal ammoniac rather than baking soda. The rag (Marcia refused to give up another dress!) did indeed prove to be "un-inflammable." Marcia and Aunt Wealthy decided to try the method on their laundry. Millie led the girls in their morning lessons while the laundry boiled. They were finished in time to help wring it out and hang it on the line.

The family settled into their new routine over the next few weeks. It seemed to Millie that her workload had more than doubled since Celestia Ann left, but she knew that couldn't be true because Marcia and Aunt Wealthy still did much more than she did. Marcia insisted that Millie take time each day for herself, and she spent time sitting in her swing, reading her Bible, or visiting her friends.

Celestia Ann dropped by almost every afternoon, for she missed the Keiths almost as much as they missed her. She often spent the afternoon with Millie in the kitchen, cooking and talking.

Rhoda Jane stopped by as often as her chores permitted, and while Millie had promised not to talk about religion or the Bible, Celestia Ann had made no such promise. It flowed so naturally from her that it was hard to be offended. Every time Celestia Ann talked about God, Millie prayed that the words would go straight to Rhoda Jane's heart.

"I know you love your husband," Rhoda Jane said in exasperation one day after Celestia Ann had spent a long time talking about how Reverend Lord was already praying about the next week's service. "He has an excellent mind and humane heart. But have you ever considered that if there is no God, your husband is wasting his life?"

Celestia Ann stopped kneading the dough for a moment and gazed into space. "Nope," she said, resuming the kneading. "I just can't do it."

"Can't do what?"

"I can't imagine there is no God."

"If there was a God," Rhoda Jane pushed, "don't you think there would be scientific evidence?"

Celestia Ann just shrugged. "I don't know enough about that to tell you. I know about cooking and milking and taking care of people. And I know that something has hurt your heart, Rhoda Jane. Have you ever imagined that if there is a God, He could care for you? What would it take for you to know there is a God?"

"Something impossible," Rhoda Jane said.

"A specific impossible thing, or any impossible thing?" Celestia Ann asked.

"A specific thing," Rhoda Jane replied.

"Did you ever ask God to do it?"

"No. I don't believe in prayer."

Celestia Ann just looked at her.

"Oh, all right." Rhoda Jane closed her eyes for a moment. "There. But it's not going to happen. I told you, it is impossible."

Lord, You heard her, didn't You? Millie prayed silently. *It's a prayer if she's talking to You, isn't it? Even if she doesn't really believe? Please answer Rhoda Jane! Help her to see that you love her!*

"Hello," Millie called at the Lightcaps' door. "Is anyone home?" Marcia and Aunt Wealthy had gone to Stuart's office and then to a meeting of the Ladies Society. Cyril and Don had disappeared, leaving the kindling box empty again. As soon as she noticed that the boys were missing, Millie had known where to look. The twins were fascinated by everything Gordon Lightcap said or did.

"Hello, Millie," Mrs. Lightcap said cheerily. She was putting the finishing touches on a new bonnet for Min. "You have missed them all, I'm afraid. Gordon and Joe promised to teach Cyril and Don how to shoot Joe's musket. I can't stand the noise, so they took it out to the prairie. Rhoda Jane and the little girls went along to keep them out of trouble. Pull up a chair and talk awhile. They will be getting hungry soon if I am not mistaken, and then they'll start for home."

Millie sighed. Those two boys were going to be in such trouble. Their father was very strict about all the children finishing their chores. She pulled a chair close to the door,

where the breeze blew through. The summer heat had become almost unbearable, and everyone was complaining about the dry spell. After an unusually wet spring, the sky had simply turned to brass. Ever since May, the gardens had been dying for lack of rain, and even the animals sought out patches of shade in which to sleep away the afternoons.

"I am afraid we are in for a bad season," Mrs. Lightcap said. "Gordon said the water is standing in pools in the swamp, not running to the river the way it ought to. That's the kind of water that breeds fevers. It's just like the year . . . well, never mind."

Millie knew what she had been going to say. *The year my husband died.* Mr. Lightcap had died of ague two years before the Keiths arrived, leaving his family to scrape out a meager existence in Pleasant Plains. Sometimes Mrs. Lightcap's mind seemed to follow an endless loop, starting in the present but turning always to the past — to her husband's death.

"I heard that Gordon is selling his carvings," Millie said, changing the subject.

"Signs, really," Mrs. Lightcap said. "It all came from the sign he did for the stagecoach station, you see. As soon as he hung it, Gordon started receiving inquiries. A cobbler from Detroit saw it as he passed through, and he asked Gordon to make him one. Gordy always said his future was in his hands, and I guess he was right. He's an artist, like his father was. My husband was an actor, you know, a very good actor. But he had learned smithing from his own father, and he loved working with his hands, creating things. He didn't like the heat, though, and he could hardly bear it that summer. He was out of his mind with it, there at the end. He was . . . delirious . . ."

Her voice faded. "But I shouldn't be telling you all of this. How are things at the warehouse?"

Millie's eye caught movement at the end of the road. Who would be running in this heat? As the figure came closer, she made out Joe Roe's long, loping stride. Hadn't he gone with the boys? Joe stopped in the street, apparently gasping for air.

"Excuse me just a moment, Mrs. Lightcap," Millie said, standing up. "I'll be right back." Millie knew something was wrong before she even reached him. He was panting for breath, and there were red spots sprayed across his white shirt.

"Joe, what is it? Are the boys all right?"

"He's near dead," Joe said between gasps.

"Who?" Millie grabbed his arm.

"Gordon. He's hurt awfully bad, Millie, almost killed. He was ramming the wadding and shot in the old musket, and the powder went off. The ramrod went clean through his chest. He bled a lot, and I couldn't stop it. They are bringing him now. Rhoda Jane told me to get things ready, but you can do that. I gotta go back and help."

"Millie?" Mrs. Lightcap called. "Is everything all right?" Millie walked quickly back into the house.

"Oh, Mrs. Lightcap," she said, "Gordon has been badly hurt." Mrs. Lightcap grabbed the back of the chair. "He is not dead," Millie said. "They are bringing him home."

Mrs. Lightcap sank into the chair, but Millie couldn't stand still. *I've got to get things ready. Where will they put Gordon when they get here?* His cot was almost impossible to reach in the lean-to part of their small, cramped quarters. The doctor, who would surely be summoned, would not be able to attend him there. Millie pulled the trundle from under Rhoda Jane's bed and dragged it to a clear space that was closer to the stove. She stripped off Rhoda Jane's bedding and threw it in the corner, then she spread towels and empty flour sacks on the mattress.

Millie could see them now, at the foot of the road. Gordon was on his feet, with Rhoda Jane on one side and Joe supporting him on the other. His feet didn't seem to be working very well. Emmaretta struggled along beside him, dragging the heavy musket by the barrel.

They stopped at the porch, and Millie ran to help. Gordon was drenched in blood. One arm was around Rhoda Jane's shoulders, the other was tucked inside the apron she had wrapped around him, holding the end of the ramrod where it entered his chest. The other end of the rod protruded from his back. It bobbed visibly every few seconds. The rhythmic jerking of the rod could only be Gordon's heartbeat. Millie swallowed hard to keep from gagging as she helped them lift him up the steps.

Emmaretta was crying, and the tears mixed with blood were making mud on her dirty face. Millie took the gun from the little girl as she came in the door and leaned it against the wall. "Did someone send for Dr. Chetwood?"

Min nodded. "Cyril went," she said. "He was runnin'. Don ran home."

"Go find my Pappa and Mamma, Emmaretta," Millie said. "You run, too."

Millie heard a thud and turned, expecting to see Gordon on the floor, but it was Mrs. Lightcap who had fainted. Joe was standing helplessly, supporting Gordon, while Min and Rhoda Jane knelt by their mother.

"Out of my way!" Dr. Chetwood had arrived, shoving his way past Cyril and several of the town's children who had run after the doctor's cart to see what was happening.

Millie pushed Cyril outside and shut the door. They eased Gordon onto the edge of the bed Millie had prepared.

"Someone move her," Dr. Chetwood commanded, and Joe and Min pulled Mrs. Lightcap out of the way.

Dr. Chetwood stepped behind Gordon and cut the back of his shirt open from collar to waist. Gordon sat staring as the doctor pulled his wooden stethoscope from his bag and placed it against Gordon's back. He listened intently, his eyes closed.

"We're going to have to pull it out, of course," Dr. Chetwood said at last, "but it is very close to the heart, Gordon. It's going to be risky."

"No," Gordon whispered as Dr. Chetwood touched the rod.

"I don't have a choice," Dr. Chetwood said.

"Let me die."

Silent tears had been running down Rhoda Jane's cheeks, and now she sobbed out loud.

"No!" Millie said. "Why would you say such a thing?"

Gordon shook his head.

For I am the Lord, your God, who takes hold of your right hand and says to you, Do not fear; I will help you. The verse just came into Millie's brain. *Is that for Gordon, Lord? Should I say it out loud?*

"Just let me die," Gordon repeated.

"For I am the Lord, your God, who takes hold of your right hand and says to you, Do not fear; I will help you." Millie hardly recognized her own voice.

"Is that from the Bible?" Gordon asked.

"Yes," Millie said. She felt terribly shaky inside.

"Where, Millie?" Rhoda Jane pulled the Bible that Millie had given her from the shelf.

"Time is of the essence here," Dr. Chetwood said. "Can't this wait?"

"No," Rhoda Jane said, shoving the Bible at Millie. "It can't." Millie flipped to Isaiah 41:13 and handed it back to her.

"For I am the Lord, your God, who takes hold of your right hand and says to you, Do not fear; I will help you." Rhoda Jane read the words in desperation. "It's right here, Gordy." There were tears running down her face. "It's right here. Let the doctor help you, please!"

Gordon closed his eyes for a moment, then nodded. "All right."

Dr. Chetwood cut the apron and shirt away from Gordon's chest, and Millie gasped. Gordon hadn't been holding the rod at all. His right hand was impaled, pinned to his chest by the rod. The flesh was burned and swollen, and Millie could see the white of shattered bones.

Dr. Chetwood cut away the rod as gently as he could, then he pulled Gordon's hand off the remaining wood and examined it. "I should amputate."

"No. Fix my hand." Gordon looked at Millie. "Fix it before you take out the rod."

Dr. Chetwood shook his head, but he reached into his bag and started laying his surgical tools on the bed. "You are going to have to sit very still," he said. "We have no time for laudanum, and it could slow your heartbeat anyway."

Millie moved to the other side of the bed and took Gordon's left hand in hers. It was cold and still fresh with blood. Gordon blinked again and tears of pain trickled down his cheeks and onto his neck. *God, help Gordon. Please help him!* Millie wiped his tears with her bare hand. Gordon turned his head away from the doctor. He sucked in his breath as the steel cut into his flesh, and his hand tightened on hers until it hurt. Millie could do nothing but hold his hand and pray.

Finally Dr. Chetwood clipped the last of the countless stitches and wrapped the hand in gauze and bandages.

"Now, you stubborn fool, let's see if you live through the next part. I hope I didn't just waste all that work." He handed a pad of gauze to Millie. "Slap this on the wound as soon as the rod is clear, and hold it fast."

Gordon was panting now, like the dog run over by a cart that Millie had once seen, and his pupils were dilated with pain. Dr. Chetwood climbed up on the bed behind him. Gordon clenched his teeth as Dr. Chetwood took the rod in his hands.

"Ready?"

Millie nodded.

Gordon screamed as the rod came out. Millie slapped the gauze against the wound, and tried to hold it as he slumped forward onto her.

"He's passed out," the doctor said. "And that's a mercy. Just hold him a minute while I plug this hole." Millie did her best to brace him up while the doctor wrapped his chest, and listened with his stethoscope again.

"No gushing, no murmur. I think it missed the heart — but only just. It must have been touching it to move that way."

The door opened, and Stuart, Marcia, and Aunt Wealthy stepped into the room. Stuart came immediately to help, taking Gordon from Millie and laying him down on the bed. Marcia and Aunt Wealthy knelt by Mrs. Lightcap.

"Are you all right?" Stuart asked, wrapping Millie in his arms.

Millie wanted to say, no, I'm not, I'm not all right, nothing is all right, but she just leaned against him and nodded. "Do you want to go home now?" he asked. She nodded again. "Your mother and I are going to stay to help Mrs. Lightcap. Aunt Wealthy will walk you home, and we will be there soon."

Aunt Wealthy must have understood, because she walked silently beside Millie all the way up the hill. Millie opened the door and stepped inside. The little angel Gordon had carved was standing guard over the family Bible on the table by the door. Millie touched it with one bloody finger and burst into tears.

She was all cried out when Stuart came home just after sunset. Marcia was spending the night at the Lightcap home, keeping vigil over both Gordon and his mother, who was suffering from a shock to the nerves. Stuart heard the story of the accident from Cyril and Don — how Gordon had measured his powder, poured it into the barrel, prepared his wadding, and tapped it down hard, leaning over the rod as he did so.

"It went off without any fire, Pappa. Just went off," Cyril said. "I saw the blood and I said I would get the doctor. I ran as fast as I could."

"You did exactly the right thing," Stuart said. "You helped save Gordon's life. Dr. Chetwood says the rod just missed the heart," Stuart continued. "He will not be able to work for a while, but he will live. He is going to need someone to help with the horses."

"I can feed them," Cyril said. "I know how."

"I'm sure you will be a help," Stuart said. "Ru is going to take over some of the other responsibilities at the stable. Reverend Lord or I will be on hand when the stagecoach arrives."

"Is he going to be able to use his hand, Pappa?" Millie asked. "Is it going to heal?"

Stuart shook his head. "Gordon's hand is destroyed. He will be lucky to use his fingers at all. His thumb may work, and if it does, he will be able to pick things up." Stuart wrapped his arms around Millie again. "Dr. Chetwood told me what you did. I am very proud of you, Millie."

That evening when Aunt Wealthy and Millie prepared the children for bed, Millie found Don curled in a dark corner of the parlor. "What's the matter, Don?" she asked, sliding down beside him. "Are you still thinking about Gordon?"

"No," Don said, "I'm thinkin' bout me. I never do the right thing, Millie. When Fan fell, I didn't catch her. If Cyril had been the one in the street he would have caught her. But I was afraid. When Gordon got hurt, I didn't run for the doctor. I ran home, because I was afraid. I'm never gonna be a longrider or a mountain man. I'm . . . I'm a coward."

"Everybody is afraid sometimes," Millie said. "Even mountain men."

Don stood up. "Well, I'm afraid 'most all the time. And now I'm afraid I'll do something wrong again."

Millie did her best to comfort him, and then headed for her own bed. She fell asleep in the middle of her prayers that night, too exhausted even to read her Bible.

⌒

"Well, Millie Eleanor Keith," Stuart said when he came home from the Lightcaps' the next day, "are you ready to bake your first birthday cake?"

"It isn't anybody's birthday," Millie said.

"Oh?" Stuart folded his arms and winked at Marcia and Aunt Wealthy. "Are you sure about that? I think the angels might disagree. They are having a party right now."

"Stuart!" Aunt Wealthy clapped her hands. "Do you mean . . ."

"I do. Gordon Lightcap is awake and sitting up. He told me about the Scripture you gave him before you even saw his hand, Millie. He said that God must have put those words in your mouth, because every single one of them went straight to his heart. He closed his eyes right then and there, before the doctor touched him, and gave his right hand to Jesus.

"Now he's had a day to think about it. He decided that he didn't want to drag someone else's hand around with him the rest of his life, so he gave the rest of himself to Jesus, too."

"You mean . . . Gordon became a Christian?" Millie couldn't believe it.

"I do, and he did. I just finished praying with him not half an hour ago."

"Pappa! That's . . . that's . . ."

"A miracle!" Aunt Wealthy said, clapping her hands again. "The angels are having a Gordon Lightcap party right now, celebrating a new baby in the Kingdom of God! And any reason good enough for the angels to throw a party is good enough for me!" Stuart twirled Millie around the table.

Millie carried a cake down to the Lightcaps' that evening. Gordon was pale but sitting up. There was a difference about him; Millie could see it even before he smiled.

"Hello, Millie," he said. "Is that for me?"

"Happy new birthday," Millie said.

Rhoda Jane took the cake and set it on the table. "Thank you," she said stiffly. Gordon shook his head.

"Rhoda Jane thinks I am just lightheaded from lack of blood," he said. "It's going to take some time to convince her that this peace and joy is real."

"How can you have peace or joy?" asked Rhoda Jane angrily. "You almost lost your hand. You will never use it again, not like before."

"But I gained a life, little sister," Gordon said gently. "A whole new life."

Mrs. Lightcap and Rhoda Jane were so uncomfortable that Millie was almost glad when Gordon changed the subject, asking after Cyril and Don. "I didn't give them too much of a fright, I hope," he said, as Rhoda Jane adjusted his pillow.

"I'm sure they will be fine," said Millie.

"And . . ." Gordon flushed. "Have you heard from Claudina?"

"No," Millie said slowly, "I have not." *Claudina has not been to visit? Surely she knows Gordon was injured.*

Rhoda Jane walked Millie to the door, but her manner was stiff and cold.

"Your mother is able to care for Gordon now," said Millie. "You should come over for tea."

"No," Rhoda Jane said flatly. "I'm sure I have too much to do. And I don't think you should come around here any more. At least not to visit me."

Millie felt as if she had been slapped. "Rhoda Jane, I . . . Why?"

"Because it wasn't fair using religion on Gordon when he was hurt and not thinking straight."

A Dangerous Recipe

Millie remembered how Rhoda Jane herself had insisted on reading aloud the Bible verse that seemed to help Gordon in his pain and hopelessness. "I didn't *use* religion. God was there for Gordon and—"

"Good-bye, Millie." Rhoda Jane shut the door.

Millie's heart ached as she walked home. *The angels might be having a party, but I am not. I can't bear it! I did and said the things You wanted me to, Lord. But now, I've lost my best friend.*

CHAPTER

9

Perfectly Safe

*Now leave this land at once
and go back to your
native land.*

GENESIS 31:13

ordon was not able to attend church that Sunday, but Millie saw Claudina Chetwood sitting in the pew with her parents. Millie had seen Dr. Chetwood's carriage in front of the Lightcaps' every day, but she had never seen Claudina get out of it. *There must be a very good reason. Surely Claudina would have gone to see Gordon if she could.*

When Claudina saw Millie looking at her, she dropped her eyes and twisted the gloves in her lap. Helen and Lu stayed close to her side most of the morning.

"Are you coming to the Big Yellow House for dinner?" Millie asked after church when she was finally able to catch Claudina alone. "I really need someone to talk to."

"No." Claudina wouldn't meet her eye. "I . . . I can't, Millie. It's too close to Gordon's house. He might see me and . . ."

"So, your parents have forbidden you to see him, then?"

"It . . . it's not that. My father said that Gordon was *maimed*. That he will be a cripple for the rest of his life."

"A terrible tragedy," Helen said, pushing her way into the conversation. "Gordon had such a talent for carving. My father said he could become an artist, possibly even a famous sculptor. Now he is never going to be anything but a hostler at a livery stable."

"You don't know that! Gordon gave his life to Jesus," Millie said. "Did you know?"

"I'm very glad that he did, but I don't want to see him broken and twisted, Millie." Claudina was weeping now. "I can't!"

Millie could feel her temper rising. "The Bible says that love is patient and kind. It hopes all things, believes all things, endures all things." Claudina was crying harder, but Millie couldn't stop. "Jesus would—"

"I'm sure He would," Helen said. "But then, Jesus loves everybody. You told me so yourself. Even cripples. But that doesn't mean you would want to be married to one."

"The Bible—"

"Don't you have any pity, Millie Keith?" Helen asked, putting her arms around Claudina. "Can't you see her heart is breaking? Why don't you go talk to Damaris Drybread? She loves to argue about what the Bible says. Come on, Claudina."

Millie was seething inside as they walked away. She suddenly knew what it was that made Cyril throw snowballs and rocks. There was something wrong with the world, something wrong in her friends, and she wished she could knock it out of them.

Dinner at the Keiths' was very subdued. Millie followed Aunt Wealthy up the stairs and into her room after the kitchen was cleaned.

"Millie!" Aunt Wealthy said, turning around. "Just the person I wanted to see. Sit down, dear. I need to talk to you." She patted the bed beside her. "We have been in Pleasant Plains for a year," Aunt Wealthy began, and Millie's heart sank.

"You can't be leaving us, Aunty! Please tell me that is not what you are going to say. I couldn't bear it just now."

"I know," Aunt Wealthy said, brushing tears from Millie's face. "I don't know how I can bear it myself. I was going to tell you days ago, but then Gordon was hurt, and I thought it best to wait. I believe the time the Lord has

allowed me to stay here is done. You and your sisters are all
helping your mother now, and Fan is better. She hasn't had
a seizure in a long time."

"You could stay at least until we move into the new house."

"No, I really can't. The young pastor who has been rent-
ing my house has been called to a church in Chicago. It is
a wonderful thing for him, to be sure, but I must go put my
things in order. I didn't know how long I was going to stay
in Pleasant Plains when we arrived, but I have been praying about it for some time, and I know His plan is for me to
leave. It's time for me to go home."

"We . . . I can't do without you!"

"I will be leaving part of my heart," Aunt Wealthy said,
wiping away another tear. "All of my grandchildren are
dear to me, but you are my special one, Millie. I am so
proud of the way you are growing in the Lord."

The tears welling in Millie's eyes made the room waver,
and she blinked to clear her vision. "You've told Mamma
and Pappa, then?"

"No, dear. I wanted to tell you first. May I pray for
you?" Millie laid her head on Aunt Wealthy's shoulder.
"Lord," Aunt Wealthy began, "I thank You for the courageous spirit You have put into Millie. I pray that You
would increase her courage and let her live totally for You,
whether her life is long or short; let every day, every breath
be for Your glory alone." She took Millie's face in her
hands and looked into her eyes. "You will have some hard
times in the next few years, dear, because growing up is
never easy. Just remember that your whole job is this: to
grow in favor with God—to walk in His ways and love others as Jesus did. I want you to know that you are doing a
very good job of this."

"Thank you, Aunt Wealthy," Millie whispered. She didn't feel as if she were doing a good job. She felt like a baby who just wanted to crawl up in her aunt's lap and sob.

"How can we do without you?" Stuart asked, when Aunt Wealthy informed the family of her decision later that night.

"Every single one of us needs you every day!" Marcia said.

"Pish-tosh," Aunt Wealthy said, although her eyes were dim with unshed tears. "You'll have each other and will soon find out that you can get on very well indeed without your eccentric old aunt. The real question is what I will do without you."

"But why must you go?" Zillah asked. "You could just live with us forever!"

"There's business I have to attend to," Aunt Wealthy said.

"You'll come back soon, won't you, Aunty?" pleaded Adah.

"Not very soon, I'm afraid. It's a long and expensive journey."

"Too long for you to take alone, Aunty," Marcia said. "I don't see how we can let you go without a protector."

"I'll protect her," said Cyril, who had been quiet the whole time, standing up. "I'll go with her and protect her."

"Thank you, dear," Aunt Wealthy said. "I know you would be a wonderful protector. But I already have one, you see. God promised me, 'I am with you and will watch over you wherever you go.' "

"How are we supposed to live here if God goes with you?" Cyril asked.

"There is another promise in the Bible, Cyril," Aunt Wealthy said. " 'I will never leave you nor forsake you.'

That means He will be right here with you, just as He is with me."

Cyril scratched his head. "Sounds s'spicous to me."

"I cannot tell you how hard it is for me to leave you all," Aunt Wealthy said, her voice trembling with emotion.

"Will you take the stagecoach?" Ru asked at last. Millie could tell he was trying to sound manly and indifferent, but his voice squeaked.

"Yes," replied Aunt Wealthy, "the very next stage, I think. I don't have much to pack."

Aunt Wealthy had always been very dear to Millie, but now that she was about to lose her, it seemed that she had never realized how much she loved her "eccentric old aunt."

For the next few days Adah, Zillah, and Fan lingered near Aunt Wealthy, hanging on her words and looks. Don sat quietly beside her, no matter what she was doing. Cyril pretended he didn't care, spending as much time at the stable with Gordon as possible. Ru helped Aunt Wealthy map out the route of the new stagecoach road.

"You should be safe from robbers and that lot," Ru said. "It is not as if there are bank boxes carried on the stage. Pleasant Plains is not a rich town."

"That is too bad," Aunt Wealthy said with feeling. Marcia stopped sewing to look at her. "About Pleasant Plains, I mean," Aunt Wealthy said quickly. "Honestly, Marcia, you worry too much. It is not as if I plan to travel the countryside like a vagabond, seeking out high adventure. I'm taking a perfectly safe stagecoach over a perfectly safe road, to a perfectly safe town where I have lived in perfect safety for many years."

Millie's Courageous Days

The Keiths all walked down to the stagecoach station to see Aunt Wealthy on her way. Wannago danced merrily among the children, except for when he was picked up and carried by Adah or Zillah, and then he washed their tear-stained faces with his tongue. Cyril walked along silent and grim.

When the stagecoach was finally loaded, Stuart helped Aunt Wealthy in and she sat down, holding Wannago close to her heart.

"Wait!" Cyril yelled, jumping in and throwing himself on her and sobbing without words.

"I love you, too, Cyril," she said, giving him a kiss. Stuart took Cyril in his arms and climbed down, and the driver shut the door.

"Good-bye, my dears," Aunt Wealthy called, "good-bye!" Millie ran along the road waving as long as it was possible and then returned to her family. The parting reminded Millie of another parting the year before, when she had left her friends in Lansdale. She couldn't quite decide which was more horrible — being the one leaving or the one left behind.

"It feels like a funeral," Adah sobbed. "Like we will never see Aunty again."

"Perhaps we will," said her mother, wiping away her own tears. "I know Aunt Wealthy goes where God sends her. Perhaps He will send her to us again. Still, I will feel more secure after I have received a letter saying she is safe in her own home."

"That reminds me," Ru said, slapping his hand to his forehead, "there's a letter in the post office for you, Mamma. I saw it there, but I had no money with me to pay the postage. If you'll give me two shillings, I'll run and get it now."

Perfectly Safe

On his return, Ru handed the letter to his mother. "It's postmarked Detroit," he said. The letter was a single page, carefully folded and sealed with wax. "I can't think who'd be likely to write to any of us from there, unless it might be Captain or Edward Wells."

"The handwriting looks familiar," Marcia said, breaking the seal and opening the sheet. "Horace Dinsmore!" she exclaimed.

Ru groaned. "Is that all? I was hoping for someone exciting." Horace Dinsmore, Jr. had visited briefly the year before the Keiths left Lansdale, and Ru had declared him a moody, self-absorbed man who had an aversion to fun and read somber books and even more somber poetry.

"He is coming to visit us!" Marcia said, quickly looking over the page. "And he could be here in a couple of weeks. Do you think we will be in the new house, Stuart? I don't think we have room here, even with Aunty gone."

"We could let him stay here, and we'll move to the new house," Zillah offered hopefully.

"Hmmmm," Stuart said. "That is very hospitable, Zillah, but I think we will be able to entertain him more appropriately if we are on the same side of town. What a pity that Aunt Wealthy missed him."

"That is a pity," Marcia agreed. "But he may be planning to stop in Lansdale on his way home from visiting us."

"Mamma, who is Horace Dinsmore?" asked Fan, who had some trouble remembering the people they had known in Lansdale. "Is he the one with the funny nose?"

"No, dear. The one with the funny nose was the milkman, Mr. Jergen. Horace is my cousin. His mother and mine were sisters."

"Were?" asked Cyril with a puzzled look. "Aren't you sisters anymore after you die?"

"Yes, dear," sighed Marcia. "But both our mothers died so many years ago that it's easier to speak of them in past tense. My mother died first. Her younger sister, my Aunt Eva, married a young man named Mr. Dinsmore and went away down South to live."

"Down South? Where people keep slaves?" Don's mouth dropped open.

"Yes," Marcia said. "Close your mouth before a fly gets in. The Dinsmores live in the South where people keep slaves. But you must remember that there are good people in the South, too. And there are people who would be good, if they knew how. But wait until I have read the letter again, and then you may ask all the questions you wish." She scanned the written words. "Cousin Horace has graduated from college and is taking a tour to rest and refresh himself after many months of hard study," she said. "He was in Detroit when he wrote this. We can expect him in two weeks. Now, what were those questions?"

"I know you met him before he visited us last time," Zillah said. "I remember you told us so, but I don't know when."

"Horace was the only child of his mother, and quite young when she died. I was there on a visit at the time, and I did what I could to comfort him. We grew very fond of each other and have been so ever since, although we have lived far apart."

"Hasn't he got a father?" asked Cyril.

"Yes, Horace has a father, and he lives with him when he is at home, but for the past few years, he's been away at college."

"I thought Cousin Horace had brothers and sisters," Ru said. "I'm sure he talked about them last year. Called them little rotters."

"I don't remember him using the word 'rotters', and I don't think you should either," Marcia said. "But yes, his father remarried and has a large family by his second wife, though the children are much younger than Horace."

"I don't want him to visit," Cyril said. "He wasn't any fun at all last year."

"Perhaps we can teach him to have fun this year," Marcia said gently.

CHAPTER

10

Foamin' Mad

Though one may be overpowered,
two can defend themselves.

ECCLESIASTES 4:12

$\mathcal{T}$he expectation of Horace's visit turned out to be a blessing in disguise. There was a rush to finish the house on the hill.

Stuart had to work at his office every day, so Marcia walked with the children to the new house the next morning. She spoke with the foreman of the work crew, giving final instructions for the completion of the upper story; then she inspected the work on the grounds.

There Ru led them in a grand tour. He had been working on the grounds and garden since the snow was off the hill, and with the help of his father, he had made some wonderful progress.

"We will begin here," Ru said importantly as they gathered on the back porch. "Notice the new henhouse across the yard." The henhouse had been up for some weeks, as had the stable, but it was awaiting the arrival of the Keiths before Stuart would buy hens. It had become a pirate fort for Don, Cyril, and Fan, where they played while Ru worked on his garden and Millie read in her swing. Millie made a mental note to have Cyril take down the skull and crossbones he had hoisted on a pole before the chickens — or Cousin Horace — arrived.

"The garden you have all seen, of course," Ru said, leading them past it. He had reason to be proud of his garden. It cascaded down the hill behind the house. He had done much of the work himself, persuading Gordon and Joe to help him with the terracing of the hill. The wet spring weather had helped in establishing the new plants. While many of the gardens of Pleasant Plains had grown withered and scorched, Ru had hauled endless buckets of water up

the hill to his, and as a result the Keiths had been eating homegrown vegetables for two weeks.

Millie followed the group down the stone steps Stuart had created to the spring by the river. This was Ru's final destination—workmen had just completed the springhouse and arbor.

"It's beautiful," Marcia said. In some places the berry bushes grew almost to the river's edge, but in others there were meadowlike spots for picnicking. The river itself, though reedy and marshy at some points, had one perfect bank for swimming. Stuart had already promised Ru a boat and a pier to tie it to.

"Can we move yet?" Don asked.

"Not quite," Marcia said. "We have waited so long for our wonderful house, we can wait a few more days. The workmen are almost done."

"I can't wait," Zillah groaned. "I want my own room."

It was Stuart who brought up the subject again three days later, just after he came home from work. "It is getting a little crowded in here, don't you think?"

"It has been crowded for a year," said Marcia.

"That is true. But the children are growing so large, I fear we will burst the seams of this poor old warehouse. We need elbow room. When shall we move, wife?"

"Tonight!" Fan said.

"Night, night, night!" Annis echoed, bouncing up and down. She had no idea what they were talking about, but if Fan was excited, then Annis was, too.

Marcia laughed. "It is not so easily done, children. I think we may begin tomorrow."

"Oh, can't we sleep there tonight?" Zillah pleaded. "We have been waiting so long!"

Stuart whispered in Marcia's ear. She looked at the children, her gaze traveling from Annis playing on the blanket, pausing with a brief wrinkle of her brow on Don and Cyril, who were holding their breath, and resting at last on Millie.

"Wel-l-l-l," she said, "I don't —"

"Please, Mamma." Cyril fell dramatically on his knees before her, his hands clasped before him. "Not thy will, but his be done!" he pleaded.

"What's that supposed to mean?" Don asked.

"It's biblical-like," Cyril said, never taking his eyes from his mother's face. "I been reading my Bible dee-voutly, and it has brought changes upon me, yea verily."

"You don't even know what Pappa said," Don pointed out.

"Whatever it was, it was good," Cyril said. "I can tell by the look in Mamma's eye."

"She looks worried to me," remarked Zillah.

"That's what I mean," Cyril hissed. "Now hush up and let her decide."

Stuart was having a hard time containing his mirth, and Marcia could not help but smile. "Well . . . all right," she said.

"All right what?" Cyril yelled, leaping to his feet.

"The children may move into the new house tonight," Stuart said. A cheer went up from the little Keiths. "Your mother and I will stay here and pack the house. We will move over when we are done."

"You mean we will stay there alone?" Ru asked.

"For one or two nights," Marcia said. "I think you and Millie can handle it. The Lords' house is not far away, and I'm sure they would be willing to help with any problems."

Cyril, Don, and Fan exploded into an impromptu war dance.

"Ahem," Stuart said, loudly enough to break through the pandemonium. The dancers stopped to gaze up at him. "Verily, I say unto you," he said, looking Cyril straight in the eye and folding his arms, "that if you do not mind your sister Millie, you will be smitten both hip and thigh."

"Yes, Pappa," Cyril said with a gulp.

"Now go pack your things."

Zillah, Adah, and the younger children thundered up the stairs.

"Will you be able to take care of Annis?" Marcia asked, a little bit of worry still in her voice.

"Of course," Millie said. "Celestia Ann is just minutes away, as Pappa said."

"And Miss Drybread's house is not much farther," Stuart added. This last comment did not comfort Millie in the least, but she said, "We'll be fine, Mamma. Ru and I can handle it."

The young Keiths packed up bedrolls and victuals. Don, Cyril, and Fan insisted on tying their belongings in handkerchiefs and hanging them from poles over their shoulders. They dressed for the journey in their coonskin caps and moccasins. Don let Fan wear his cap and tied a red kerchief on his head instead, looking like a mix between a gypsy and a pirate king. He decided he had to take his stores of marbles, a slingshot, bits of twine, a broken knife, a few fishhooks, and a set of jackstraws his father had made for him.

"You're not going to need all that stuff," said Ru. "You can come back for it tomorrow."

Don just shook his head. "I'll feel better if I know where it is," he said.

Fan decided she would take her treasures also, which consisted of some of her dolls and their wardrobes, a pic-

turebook, and some badly battered and bruised dishes, the remains of a once highly-prized metal toy tea set. What they couldn't carry in their arms was stowed in the nursery wagon, leaving just enough room in the corner for Annis.

"Wait!" Fan cried as Millie tucked the baby into the wagon. She ran back inside and came out carrying the carved wooden angel Gordon had given her. "I'll lead the way," she said.

And so she did, in moccasins, pantalets, a neat white apron, and a coonskin cap, holding an angel proudly in front of her.

The caravan gained members as they went—Emmaretta and Min joined them at the foot of the hill. Millie looked wistfully for Rhoda Jane, but she was nowhere in sight. When they reached the house on the hill, the children put their bedrolls in their various rooms. Millie set her bedding and that of Annis's in her room, and she went downstairs to prepare supper. Although the upstairs was still bare, the downstairs rooms had been finished and in order since Celestia Ann's wedding, with the chairs and tables and dishes just waiting for the arrival of the Keiths.

Millie kept Annis with her in the kitchen, but she allowed the other children to play in the garden with Emmaretta and Min.

Ru set a fire in the cookstove, and Millie boiled water for tea. She soon wished she hadn't, as the stove made the kitchen unbearably hot, and there was nothing for it but to let the fire burn down. Millie opened the window by the table to let the air flow through, then she set out the cold sandwiches her mother had sent for their supper. Ru said the prayer before their first meal in the new house.

Millie's Courageous Days

By the time Millie had cleaned the dishes and put the kitchen in order, fireflies were lighting up the soft dusk of evening.

"Do you think we should light the lamp, Ru?" asked Millie.

"Lamp!" Ru smacked his forehead. "I knew we were forgetting something. I didn't pack one, Millie, did you?"

"No," Millie said. "And no candles either. And we will be needing light in a few moments, I'm afraid."

"I'll run to the Big Yellow House and bring them," Ru said. "It won't take long."

Millie gathered the children on the porch, where the evening light was still soft, to wait for Ru's return.

"Will you read to us, Millie?" asked Zillah.

"I will when Ru gets back with a light."

"Oh," Zillah said, drawing her knees up to her chin. "I need a book to distract me."

"Distract you from what?" Millie asked.

"Min said this hill was an Indian burial ground," Adah said.

"Yeah," Don piped in. "She said a warrior named Bloody Joe swore to take vengeance on anyone who bought this land."

"He stalks by night," Cyril whispered, "seeking scalps."

"That's nonsense," said Millie, as a shiver went down her spine. "You know better than to listen to that kind of story. What would Mamma say?"

"How do you know it *isn't* true?" Fan asked in a very small voice.

"Because," Millie said, "I know what *is* true—the Word of God. And doesn't the Bible say that a great gulf separates the living from the dead? Remember the rich man who

wanted to come back to warn his brothers not to sin? What did God tell him?"

"That he couldn't come back," Zillah said.

"That's right. Now if God would not let that man come back to warn his brothers, why would He let someone come back to wreak vengeance?"

"Don't guess he would," Cyril said, but he backed up to Millie and stared out at the gathering darkness.

"And didn't God promise to take care of us?" Millie asked. Just then, way down the hill they saw a lantern bobbing along.

"There's Ru," Millie said. "When he gets here, I will read you a story from the Bible."

Ru arrived with lantern, lamp, and candles. Millie led the children into the sitting room, and they sat around her on the floor as she read to them about Joshua and the Promised Land.

No more mention was made of ghosts, and by the time Millie was done reading, Annis was sound asleep on Ru's lap, and Fan and Cyril were yawning.

Millie took them upstairs and tucked each one into a bedroll, and she listened as they said their prayers.

Ru had laid Annis, fast asleep, on Millie's bedding. Millie lay down beside the baby and fluffed her pillow. A gentle breeze was stirring on the hilltop, swaying through the branches of the old trees in the yard and whispering in the eaves.

Thank You for our new house, Millie prayed. *I love every bit of it.* She made sure a candle stub and matches were near at hand in case she needed them in the night. She blew out the lantern and the room went dark. She was so tired that she couldn't keep her eyes open another minute.

Suddenly someone burst into the room. "Millie?" It was Cyril. "Can I sleep in here with you? I'm scared."

Millie groaned, but she made room for him to stretch his bedroll out beside hers.

Zillah was the next to appear, with Fan in tow. "We heard something," she said. "A real something moving around outside."

"It was probably the wind," Millie said, and she moved over again.

"No, it wasn't." Cyril was sitting up. "I heard it, too. It was something scratching at a window. Don heard it, too, but he just put the blanket over his head. He said he was too scared to move." Millie sighed. Adah was the next to appear, and then Ru, looking sheepish.

"I thought you might need some help with the young ones," he said, trying to make his voice low like his father's.

"Are you sure there's no such thing as ghosts?" Cyril asked.

"I'm sure," Millie said.

"How 'bout hydrophoby skunks?" Cyril asked.

"Yeah," said Fan. "It could be a hydrophoby skunk."

Everyone was looking at Millie for reassurance now.

"Oh, for heaven's sake!" she said, standing up. "I'm going to show you that there is nothing down there. It's just the wind." Millie lit her candle stub. The light filled the room with flickering shadows, but it seemed to comfort the children. She marched to the doorway and waited, looking out into the darkness of the hallway. For a moment everything was silent as the children held their collective breath. "See?" Millie said. "I told you . . ." and then there came an unmistakable thump, and a scraping sound. There *was* something down there. Zillah started to cry.

Foamin' Mad

"What should we do, Millie?" asked Ru.

Millie looked at her younger brothers and sisters huddled in the middle of the floor. Was this the way a shepherd felt when a wolf came prowling round his sheep? *Mamma and Pappa are trusting me to take care of them, Lord. Help me be brave,* she prayed.

"I'm going to see what it is. All of you stay here—and keep this door shut," she said with emphasis as she pulled it shut behind her. As she started for the stairs, she saw the door to Don's room open, and she could see his bedding on the floor inside. *Why hadn't he come in with Cyril? It would be better than being all alone in the dark . . . Bloody Joe, Bloody Joe, Bloody Joe.* "That's ridiculous," she said. It was her own heartbeat pounding in her ears, not words or whispers. She walked slowly down the stairs. The scratching sounds were coming from the kitchen. *Please don't let there be anything there.* Millie stepped into the room, and her heart nearly stopped. At the top of a huge dark shape on the other side of the room, two fierce red eyes were shining bright as coals in the candlelight. Millie gasped, and the candle went out. She fumbled in her pocket for the matches, struck another, and lit the candle again. The huge shape revealed itself to be a chair, and on it was perched a large raccoon. The curtain behind it flapped at the window through which it had come, the breeze making the candle flame flicker again.

"Get out!" Millie said. "Shoo!" The raccoon hissed at her and bared its fangs, shaking its head back and forth as if it were having trouble seeing. What was wrong with the beast? It shook its head again and started down the chair, snarling.

The hair on Millie's neck stood up. *Hydrophobia? One bite means death.* She grabbed the broom she had left leaning against the wall in one hand and held the candle in the

other. *The children are upstairs. That raccoon must not get past me. It must not.* The raccoon took another step. Millie gripped the broom and tried to shelter the candle at the same time. If the light went out, she wouldn't be able to see where the creature was. *Lord, help me!*

Twang, thwack! The raccoon jumped and spun around. *Twang, ping!* Something ricocheted off the stove.

"Hold still, Millie, I need the light!" came Don's voice from somewhere behind her.

The candle flickered in the breeze. *Don't let it go out, God,* Millie prayed.

Twang, thwack! This time the raccoon turned and headed for the window. It jumped on the chair, grabbed the curtain, climbed onto the windowsill, and jumped outside. Millie rushed across the room and slammed the window shut. Then she turned with her hand over her mouth.

Don was crouching in the doorway, another marble already in his slingshot.

"I saved you, Millie," he said, with something like wonder in his voice. "I was afraid, but I came anyway. And I saved you."

"Yes, you did," Millie said, setting the candle carefully on the table before she gathered him in a big hug. "You are my hero, Donald Keith!"

Millie checked every window in the house, then she and Don returned to the bedroom to join the other children.

"I don't believe it was hydrophobic," Ru said after he heard the story.

"It was so," Don insisted. "It was foamin' mad."

"I think I should take the lantern and . . ."

"You will not, Rupert Keith!" Millie said firmly. "You will stay inside."

"Pappa said for us to obey Millie," Zillah said.

Ru shook his head. None of the children wanted to go to their own rooms, so the bedrolls and blankets on Millie's floor were shared among them all. Millie's hero spent the rest of the night with his back against the door, his slingshot in his hand.

———

Millie kept the children inside the house until her parents arrived the next morning.

"See, I told you they were fine," Stuart said to Marcia as the children rushed at him. "Better keep a close watch on them today, though, Millie. Mr. Roe shot a raccoon this morning on his porch. He said he was sure it had hydrophobia."

"Told ya," Don said, giving Ru a look.

"Told him what?" Marcia asked. She sank slowly onto a chair and the color drained from her face as Millie told of the night's adventure.

CHAPTER 11

Taking a Stand

*Who will rise up for me against
the wicked? Who will take
a stand for me against
evildoers?*

PSALM 94:16

Taking A Stand

I know you think I am terrible. I don't blame you at all." Claudina was sitting on the bed in Millie's new room. The Keiths had finished their move and Marcia, with the girls' help, had made quick work of settling into the bedrooms. Much of Millie's time had been occupied by preparing for Cousin Horace the large comfortable room that had been intended for Aunt Wealthy, but Millie's mind was on her friends. Rhoda Jane had not come to call since the move, and Millie had been surprised to find Claudina on her doorstep that afternoon.

"I did think I was in love with Gordon, and I told him so," Claudina continued. "That's the terrible thing. I wish I had never said those words, but I can't take them back, even though I now know they aren't true. You were right, Millie. If I loved Gordon, it wouldn't matter whether or not he had a crippled hand. How am I ever going to speak to him again? I wish I could move to another town where I wouldn't have to see him."

"I don't think moving would heal your heart," Millie said slowly. "I know it wouldn't help Gordon's. Have you talked to your mother about this?"

Claudina shook her head. "I can't. She would never understand. I can't talk to anyone, not even you."

Millie's heart hurt for her friend. What could she possibly do to help? "I know someone who will keep your secrets, and talk about them only with Jesus," she said at last. "She always keeps mine. Do you think you could talk to my Mamma?"

"I think I could. I have to talk to someone or I will just explode!"

They found Marcia in the garden, loosening the soil around her rosebushes.

"Could I have a moment of your time, Mrs. Keith?" Claudina asked formally. "I . . ." A tiny sob escaped her.

"Of course, Claudina," Marcia said, taking off her garden bonnet and gloves. She drew the girl over to a bench and sat beside her. Millie stood uncertain for a moment, then, at a nod from her mother, she left them alone and walked across the garden to her swing.

Millie leaned back in the swing, pointing her toes at the sky. The swing rose higher each time she pumped, until the world was flashing by beneath her. She remembered her conversation with Claudina. *"What do you see?"*

"Gordon's house . . . I love him."

Millie looked back and saw that her mother had her arms around Claudina. Millie didn't know what she was saying, but she knew just what her mother would be doing. Loving Claudina the way Jesus would.

Millie let the swing slow and stop. Gordon's house was Rhoda Jane's house, too, and Millie missed her friend so much it hurt.

The Keiths watched the stagecoach road every day, but the room Millie had prepared for Horace sat clean and empty.

"He could be delayed by weather, just as we were," Stuart said. "Or maybe he changed his plans."

Life went on, Ru working in the garden, Stuart spending time at the office, and Marcia working with the Ladies Society.

Taking A Stand

One day when Celestia Ann had dropped by to visit and to help Millie make a pie, the knocker on the front door rapped sharply. Millie wiped her hands on her apron and went to answer it.

A dark-eyed handsome young man of distinguished appearance stood on the porch.

"Is this the Keith household?" he asked.

"Yes," Millie said, realizing that this was the long-awaited cousin. She wiped the rest of the flour from her hands, but before she could greet him properly, he brushed past her into the entry hall with the air of a prince of royal blood. "Is the family in? I assume they told you I was coming."

"Why, yes," Millie said. "I believe the oldest daughter is home." She held out her hand. "I'm Millie Keith. We met last year."

"Forgive me!" The young man flushed brightly. "I do apologize! I thought . . ."

"Never mind, Cousin Horace," Millie said kindly. "We have been waiting for you, and I'm glad you are here safe and sound. Can I help you with your bags?"

"Help me? I would never think of such a thing!" Horace exclaimed. He whistled sharply, and a young black man appeared behind him, carrying a pile of luggage.

"Where should John put my bags?" asked Horace.

"We weren't expecting you to bring a friend," Millie said slowly. "I will have to prepare another room."

"Friend?" Horace laughed. "John is not a friend, Millie. He's a slave. Just give him a blanket. He will sleep in the stable with the animals."

For one moment Millie was speechless. *A slave?*

"Of course you won't stay in the stable," Millie said, holding out her hand to John. "My name is Millie Keith.

155

I'm sure my mother would want me to set up a room for you right away."

Horace raised his eyebrows, and his lips curled in amusement. "Well, John, what do you say to that?"

"Not necessary, miss," John said without lifting his eyes. "I'll sleep on the floor in Master Horace's room."

"I think not," said Millie, her temper rising. *How dare Cousin Horace treat John in such a way!* "It would be an insult to my mother's hospitality. You wouldn't want that, would you? If you gentlemen will wait in the sitting room, I'll make up an extra room." She led the way to the sitting room and left them there.

"Celestia Ann, could you help me?" Millie asked, quickly explaining the situation. "I need to make up another room. I think we'll have to use Ru's, and he'll have to move to Cyril's."

Millie and Celestia Ann quickly changed the linens and pulled Ru's clothes from the chiffarobe.

"You're moving John in here," Celestia Ann said with approval. "It's a nice room."

"Oh, no." Millie smiled sweetly. "I'm moving Cousin Horace in here. John gets the guest room."

Celestia Ann giggled. "I like the way you think, Millie Keith."

Millie and Celestia Ann went back downstairs.

"We'll show you to your rooms now," Millie said. "This way, please." Horace stood, stretched, and picked up his hat. John picked up all the bags, carrying one under each arm and one in each hand. Millie led the way up the stairs to Ru's room.

"Here we are, Cousin," she said, opening the door.

Horace stepped inside the small room and hung his hat. "This will be marvelous." He sat on the edge of the

bed and sighed. "Thank you, cousin Millie," he said, and he seemed truly grateful for the bed. "You may unpack now, John."

John seemed expert at unpacking the bags, hanging coats and putting shirts and pants neatly in the drawers. He arranged Horace's toiletries in exact order on the dressing table, then he stood back with his head down.

"You may go, John," Horace said.

"Let me show you your room." Millie led John down the hall to the guest room. She opened the door and he stepped inside. His eyes took in the fine apartment, but there was no expression on his face.

"Thank you, miss," he said, setting down his bag.

"We will call you for dinner," Millie said.

"I'll be attending Master Horace," John replied, still expressionless. Millie left him to settle himself and went back downstairs.

Marcia and Stuart were just coming in. Millie explained about the visitors. Stuart looked pensive when she mentioned John.

"I never thought he would bring his personal slave with him," Marcia said. "I never thought!"

Stuart sat down slowly. "Well," he said. "Well, well."

"You do what you think is right, husband," Marcia said. "I will stand by you."

At that moment Horace Dinsmore came down the stairs, John following behind. Horace's face lit up at the sight of his cousin. "Marcia!"

Marcia hugged him. "Horace, it is so good to see you! You remember my husband, Stuart?"

"I do," Horace said, extending a hand. "Good to see you again."

"Good to see you, too. You have finished your studies, I'm told?"

"I have, and I hope now to travel. It seems the perfect way to complete my education."

"And you, sir," Stuart addressed John. "I welcome you to my home, also."

"Thank you, sir," John said.

"Horace, before we go any further, I must tell you that I am an abolitionist."

"I suspected as much, after meeting your daughter," Horace said. "And you are not the first I have met, sir. You understand that I have a different opinion."

"I understand that," Stuart said. "But in my home, I cannot condone slavery. In fact, I am willing to offer any price you ask for John's freedom right now." Millie saw her mother blink. She had read that black children were sold by the pound, like so much meat at the market, but a healthy, male house slave could cost eighteen hundred dollars, half the amount Pappa had spent on the new house. Millie knew that Pappa would sell the house without a second thought and move them back to the warehouse if it would buy John's freedom.

Horace looked amused. "How about it, John? I'll make him a good deal—do you want your freedom?"

Two heartbeats passed, three, and then John spoke. "No, master."

"There, you see?" Horace said. "John is perfectly content with his lot. We have been together since we were babies, John and I. His mother was my nurse."

Stuart looked a little pale. He walked to the big family Bible on the table and opened it to Galatians 3:26–28: "'You are all sons of God through faith in Christ Jesus, for all of

you who were baptized into Christ have been clothed with Christ. There is neither Jew nor Greek, slave nor free, male nor female, for you are all one in Christ Jesus.' This house belongs to Jesus, Horace, and His rule applies. In this house John will be treated exactly like any other guest. If you are not able to do this, we will find rooms for you at Mrs. Prior's boardinghouse. It is an excellent establishment, and we have stayed there ourselves."

"This gives me no difficulty," Horace said. "I hope you will find me open-minded, sir."

"And you, sir?" Stuart addressed John. John looked to Horace, who shrugged.

"I will respect your household rules, sir," John said.

For the next few days it was apparent that following the system was more difficult for John than it was for Horace. As Marcia pointed out, there was no change in Horace's social standing. He seemed to take great delight in questioning the Keiths, especially Millie, about their beliefs, and listening intently to what they had to say. Millie was just as curious about the life and thinking of someone who had grown up in the South attended by slaves.

She found very quickly that Horace was a man of integrity and honor. He had a deep pride in what he referred to as "the code of the South," and Millie was sure he would have laid down his life rather than tell a lie. He treated John with the same courtesy that he showed members of the family, but no matter what she said, or what argument she used, she could not change his mind about slavery.

John was equally as fascinating, although Millie had few opportunities to speak to him alone. She took one of the opportunities when he was helping Ru with the garden to ask the question that had been bothering her since their arrival.

"Pappa offered to buy your freedom," she said. "Why on earth didn't you take it?"

"There's more than one chain that can hold a man. My mother and father are both slaves back at the Roselands Plantation. If I accept my freedom I will never see 'em again. If I traveled south, I would be taken for a runaway slave. Even if I had my papers, stating that I was free, they would just burn them. I would be sold to another plantation, maybe one of the death plantations way down south, where they wear a man out in five years, and when they bury his body they buy another to take his place." John shook his head. "Freedom is a beautiful dream. But I don't want that dream without my family. I want to take 'em with me."

Millie didn't want to like Horace, but she found that she did. He was certainly changed for the better since his last visit, and he showed much interest in them and their affairs — from Cyril's mischief to Annis's simple words, although he seemed more reticent with Annis than he was with the other children. Millie saw him more than once turn away from watching the little girl with troubled shadows in his eyes, and she wondered what could be causing his pain.

John joined the family on every excursion they planned for Horace's entertainment, from boating to picnics, and although he was openly accepted by the Keiths, his presence caused consternation in the community. The first Sunday he attended church with them, his appearance caused a stir. Reverend Lord and Celestia Ann welcomed both Horace and John warmly, but several members of the small congregation stood up and left the building when

they saw John sitting with the Keiths. Wallace Ormsby was more concerned with the handsome stranger who sat beside Millie. He gave him several long looks during the sermon and didn't relax even when Horace was introduced as a cousin.

When the Keiths returned from church they found that a window on the front of their house had been smashed. A large rock lay on the floor in the midst of the broken glass. It had a paper wrapped around it, which Stuart read and then put in his pocket.

"What does it say?" Ru asked.

"Never mind," Stuart said.

"I'm sorry, Stuart," Horace said. "I really am. I believe people should be allowed to live as they see fit, and I can't stand closed-mindedness."

The next Sunday the church was more full than usual, with people coming to gawk at John as if he were a spectacle. Millie shivered when she remembered the stories of abolitionists stoned, their homes burned to the ground. But Marcia and Stuart just smiled politely at everyone, no matter what they said. *How can they be so friendly? Don't they realize that it was most likely someone sitting in these pews who threw the rock through our window?* thought Millie.

One day after Horace had been with them for several weeks, Millie was walking with him beside the river.

"Do you really believe what you said the afternoon someone broke our window?" she asked. "About people living as they see fit?"

"I do," Horace said. "Your father has the right to run his household as he chooses. It is abominable to me that your neighbors would destroy your property because of your views."

"What about the slaves?" Millie said. "Do you believe they have the right to live as they choose? Or do you believe they are not people?"

"Touché," Horace said, and he smiled. "You know you have a fine mind for a girl. Are you pursuing your education? I think several of the young men around here have noticed how special you are."

"You are changing the subject," Millie said. "I asked if you believe that slaves should have the right to live as they choose. And do you consider them people?"

Horace walked for a time without speaking. "No," he said at last. "I don't think they should be able to choose. I don't think they are capable. If they did not have the plantations to employ them and overseers to make them work, I believe they would starve."

"You believe."

"I could be wrong." Horace picked up a stone and skipped it across the water. "I've been wrong about several things lately. More wrong than I could have believed possible. That's one of the reasons I have decided to travel. To see the world from a different perspective." They walked on in silence for some time, finally turning their steps toward home.

"Mamma, my head hurts," Zillah said as she stood up from playing with her tea set. "I want to lie down." Marcia felt her brow and frowned.

"You seem a bit hot. Maybe you should rest in the cool of your room." She was no sooner in bed than Adah was complaining of headache and chills. Dr. Chetwood was summoned, and he diagnosed ague.

"We have not much sickness here except for ague," he remarked, pulling a bottle of quinine from his black bag. "There are several varieties of that—chills and fever occurring at regular intervals, generally every other day at about the same hour—dumb ague, shaking ague, and sinking or congestive chills. The last two are the only very alarming kinds, sometimes proving fatal in a few hours. You Keiths were fortunate not to be stricken your first year here. The children have got a very mild form and I am sure they will be fine."

But the fever lingered, increasing Marcia's workload as she took care of her sick ones and her household chores as well. Finally Horace came to Marcia.

"I think John and I must end our visit," he said. "I know what a burden company can be when there is illness in the house."

It was agreed that they would leave on the next stage, two days hence. Millie saw very little of them, as she was helping Marcia nurse the sick children. Adah was content to stay in bed, but Zillah paced the floor, now asking for a blanket, then throwing it off. Finally the fever and exhaustion forced her to sleep.

The day before he was to leave, Horace found Marcia and Millie in the sitting room, alone except for little Annis playing on the floor.

"Marcia," he said, taking a chair near her side, "there is something I must tell you before I go. I came with the purpose of doing so, but my heart has failed me."

"I will leave you two alone," Millie said, rising.

"No, stay," Horace said. "I am certain that you are not of a faint disposition, and if my story could be a caution to you . . . stay. That is, if you will allow it?" he asked, turning to Marcia.

Marcia looked at him intently, then nodded. "I can't imagine you have done anything wrong, Horace. Millie may stay."

"And, Marcia, please share what I am about to tell you with Stuart. If he were not at the office today, I would have wanted him here to hear it, too," added Horace.

Horace did not speak again for a few minutes, but sat watching Annis with the same peculiar expression Millie had noted before.

"What is it you see in my baby, Horace?" Marcia asked, laying her hand affectionately on his arm.

"She is a sweet, pretty little thing. It gives me more pain than pleasure to look at her." He sighed and rubbed his hand across his eyes. "There is a page in my life that you have not read," he went on, "because it has been torn out by my father." He stood and paced across the room to the window.

"You needn't tell us, if it causes you pain," Marcia said.

"If I don't speak to someone about it, I will die!" he said with sudden determination. "I . . . I have been a husband, Marcia. I am a father."

"Horace, you are just twenty years old!" Marcia looked at him in utter amazement.

"I've never seen my little girl," he said. "She must be about the age of Annis."

"How could I not have heard of your marriage?" Marcia asked.

Horace nodded, and took a deep breath. "I knew you would be upset. I want you to hear the whole story from me, before you hear anything from my father. Three years ago, on a visit to New Orleans, I met a beautiful Christian girl, named Elsie Grayson. She was two years older than

Millie is now, in fact. That's why I asked you to stay, Millie. You have that rare beauty, inner beauty, if you will, that my Elsie did. If my story can save you some future hurt . . ." He resumed his pacing. "Elsie was an orphan, and very much alone. I convinced her to run away and marry me."

"Horace! When she was fifteen! Just a child!"

"I know, Marcia. You cannot condemn me more than I now condemn myself. But I was mad with love. We were happy — blissfully happy — for a few months . . . but when my father discovered our marriage, he arrived with the constables and her guardian. They pulled Elsie from my arms, put her in the carriage and forbade us to ever see each other again." His voice cracked. "She believed in me. Trusted me. But I couldn't keep her safe."

"Perhaps I can talk to your father," Marcia said.

Horace shook his head. "Elsie died at the end of that year . . . a week after giving birth to our daughter. They named the baby after her," he said with a shaky voice. "Marcia, if I had known, if anyone had told me . . . I would have fought my way through hell to be at her side. But I didn't know. I thought we would be together again, if I only waited . . ."

"My poor cousin!" Marcia said. "Why didn't you tell me before?"

"I could not. This is the first time I have spoken Elsie's name since . . . since I knew that she was lost to me forever."

"Forever? You said she was a sweet Christian girl, and no one who trusts in Jesus can ever be lost."

"She's lost to me. I am no Christian, and can never become one. What kind of God would want a man who abandoned his wife?" Horace asked as he turned his face from them.

"You never abandoned her," Millie said. "They took her away."

"But I let them."

After a few moments, Marcia spoke. "Where is your child, Horace?"

"She lives with her mother's guardian at a plantation called Viamede not far from New Orleans. I have never seen her."

"How can you bear it?" Millie whispered. "Don't you long to hold her?

"No," Horace said, and now his voice was harsh. "She robbed me of my wife."

"No!" Marcia said. "It was not the baby's fault. You must know that."

"I know it in my head, but I can't help my feelings. I almost hate her."

"I can't believe it of you," Marcia insisted. "Poor mother-less baby, and almost fatherless, too."

"What would you have me do, Marcia?" he asked, his face still turned away but his voice softened. "I do not know how to raise a child. She is well off where she is, under the care of a pious old Scottish woman who has been the house-keeper for the Grayson family for many years, and that of the nursemaid—a slave," he said, glancing cautiously at Millie, "who served her mother before her. They believe in Jesus just like you do. Besides, what could I give her—a life of wandering with a man who wishes he were in the grave with his beloved?"

"Forgive me if I have seemed harsh," Marcia said with tears in her eyes, "but my heart aches over that poor baby! And for you." She put her hand on his arm. "I can't mend broken hearts. But there is One who can. You said your beloved was a Christian. If you ask Him to, I know He can do something wonderful for you and your little Elsie."

"Don't call her that!" Horace put his head in his hands. "My Elsie, the most beautiful, sweetest creature on earth, is dead."

Marcia folded him in a hug. "You barely knew your own mother, Horace, because she died so young. And I know you haven't gotten on well with your stepmother. So I am going to do a mother's duty for you. I will pray every day for you and your sweet baby, until you find your way home to her." Horace's shoulders shook, and he tried to disguise his sobs. He turned away from them both again.

"Forgive me," he said. "That was unmanly of me . . ."

"Never!" Marcia said. "Stuart is the strongest man I have ever met, and I have seen him cry over his children."

Horace wiped his eyes. "I am afraid you saw more than I intended you to, Millie. I thought my tale might serve as a caution to you, but I find I have provided a spectacle," he sighed. "Maybe that will serve even better. Guard your heart, Millie Keith."

"I have already given my heart to the One who loves me best," Millie said. "I trust He will keep it for me."

After Horace had left the room, Marcia said, "Poor Horace, he is hardly more than a boy himself, and surely not ready to be a father."

"I'll pray with you," Millie said. "For Cousin Horace and little Elsie."

That night Millie took the paper out of her Bible and added two names to the list on the back — Horace and Elsie Dinsmore. The sadness lingered in Millie's heart for long after Cousin Horace had gone, and Millie made baby Elsie a regular part of her prayers. *Don't let her be alone, Lord. And let Cousin Horace's wanderings lead him to You.*

CHAPTER

12

The Naked Truth

*Then they will call to me but I
will not answer; they will look
for me but will not
find me.*

PROVERBS 1:28

The Naked Truth

*A*dah and Zillah stayed a week more in bed, but none of the other Keiths seemed to be affected by the fever. "A blessing from the Lord," Marcia had said. "We would never get our work done otherwise." Work—and love—were the only things in endless supply at the Keith home. Millie was glad of the work, because with Cousin Horace's departure, she found herself especially missing Rhoda Jane. Claudina and Helen often came to visit, and they were pleasant enough, but Millie missed Rhoda Jane's strong opinions of books and political events. She missed the imagination and poetry. Rhoda Jane's company had made Pleasant Plains bearable until Millie had felt more at home. How could you lose a best friend? Just stop speaking or visiting?

Millie threw herself into her chores with such vigor that Stuart had to force her to go outside sometimes. Marcia felt that sunshine and fresh air and good food were necessary to health. If that were the case, Don, Cyril, and Fan were in very little danger. Each had a small garden plot to tend, as well as their own broody hens to care for. Most of the gardening and poultry care fell to Ru, as well as the maintenance of the property.

"That's enough of that," Marcia said one afternoon, wiping the sweat from her brow. "We have put up enough pickles to feed an army. I feel like having a picnic."

"Me, too!" Fan yelled.

"Too, too, too!" Annis said, clapping her hands.

Millie set about gathering sunbonnets and hats for the little ones while Marcia packed a picnic meal.

"Are you going with us, Ru?" Millie asked when he wandered through the kitchen in his overalls.

"No." Ru tucked his thumbs in his shoulders straps, and rocked on his heels. "Pappa said I could paint the new shed today. He picked up the paint and brushes yesterday. Any of you fellows want to stay and help me paint?"

Cyril and Don looked at him as if he had gone crazy. "We're going on a picnic," they said, "with Mamma."

"Fine," Ru said. "I guess you will miss all the fun."

"Guess so," Cyril said, shaking his head. "'Sa shame, really, but we gotta take care of the girls."

"Yeah," Don said, edging toward the door. "We gotta take care of them."

They scooted past Millie and ran for the garden with Fan hard on their heels.

"I guess you lost your helpers," Marcia laughed. "But we'll be back. Are you sure you don't want to come with us?"

"There was a ring around the moon last night," Ru said, shaking his head, "and Mr. Roe said that means rain is coming. Pappa is depending on me to get it done." He went out the back door, and Marcia stood watching through the window for just a moment. "You know, Millie, I am so proud of the way you and Ru—all of you, really—have grown since we moved to the frontier. I can't imagine a boy of Rupert's age taking on the responsibilities he now has back . . ." Millie saw her mother catch herself. She had almost said "back home in Lansdale."

Pleasant Plains is home now, Millie thought. *Really home.* Moving to the frontier had changed the Keiths in many ways. Millie's own hands were sun-browned and rough from helping Ru with the garden and Mamma with the

laundry. Mamma served pies made from fruit she had canned herself. Don and Cyril spent most of their time shirtless and barefoot in overalls, although their mother insisted they wear straw hats. They fished with Gordon and spent time with Emmaretta and Min gathering nuts and berries in season. What would her friends in Lansdale think if they could see them now? *I like it, God. It's hard work, but I like it. You did have a good plan.*

"Basket's done," Marcia said. "Grab a blanket and we'll put them in Annis's wagon." Marcia settled the basket and blanket in the wagon. Annis was stomping her chubby feet in excitement, laughing with glee when her mother picked her up and put her in the wagon, too.

Adah and Zillah were waiting on the porch, but Cyril, Don, and Fan had disappeared around the house.

Fan soon came running back around the corner. "Mamma, Millie, Mamma, Millie, come see! Speckle has thirteen chicks! Thirteen!"

They pushed the wagon around the side of the house. Speckle was strutting proudly around the yard, thirteen balls of fluff following her every move.

"Eeep, eeeep," Annis said, imitating the babies. Marcia laughed and lifted her out of the wagon. Annis reached out to touch one of the chicks, but Fan pushed her finger away.

"Careful," she said. "They're babies!"

"Ohhhhh!" Annis gasped in delight as Millie shook a few crumbs on the ground and the chicks rushed after them. Marcia had to examine Adah's hen, which was still sitting on her nest, and Cyril and Don's chicks, which had hatched the week before and grown larger. After they had examined each brood they went down to the shed to say good-bye to Ru. He was standing on the top rung of his ladder, reaching

high above his head with the paintbrush. The can of paint was dangling from his other hand.

"Be careful, son," Marcia called, as he stood on tiptoe to reach the eaves.

"Don't worry, Mamma," he said, smiling over his shoulder. "I've seen Pappa do this a hundred times."

"Pappa ain't painted a hundred sheds," Cyril argued, looking up at him.

"It was a figure of speech," Ru explained. "It means I have seen Pappa do it often enough that I know how to do it myself."

At that moment the top of the ladder began to slip. "Run, Cyril!" Ru yelled, as he tried to save himself by grabbing hold of the eaves with one hand. The ladder fell, and Ru was suspended for a fraction of a second, clinging to the eaves with his fingertips, the other hand still holding the gallon of paint. And then he fell, letting go of the paint at the last moment. Ru landed on his feet, and the paint can landed beside him. The liquid inside seemed to bounce, coming up into the air with a mighty splash, covering both Ru and Cyril head to toe.

"I never seen Pappa do that," Cyril said, wiping blue paint from his face.

"Are you all right?" Marcia asked, taking a step toward Ru, then thinking better of it.

"I'm fine," Ru said. "My clothes got the worst of it. We've robbed the shed of half its new coat."

Zillah giggled and put her hand over her mouth. Annis was not so refined. She laughed in delight and clapped her hands as she gazed at her blue brothers.

"I've wasted half the can," Ru said, spreading his dripping arms. "What's Pappa going to say?"

"He'll say, 'Thank goodness my boys weren't hurt,' "
Marcia replied. "Now, you two might as well put the ladder
away and head down to the river. You can wash your
clothes out there, and wash yourselves. I don't want to be
cleaning paint off the kitchen floor."

"Waahooo!" yelled Cyril. "We're goin' swimmin'!"

Millie lifted Annis into the little wagon and pushed it
down the path, followed by Adah, Zillah, Don, and Fan.
Marcia held Fan's hand.

The sky was a dark celestial blue with here and there a
floating cloud of snowy whiteness whose shadows flitted
over the landscape, alternating light and shade. It had been
a very wet year and the grass beneath their feet was emer-
ald green, thickly studded with wild flowers of every hue.
Yellow-and-black swallowtail butterflies glided along the
path and rested in the branches of the cherry tree the
Keiths had settled under to eat their meal.

"So," Marcia said to Millie when the children ran to play.
"Do you want to talk about it?"

"Talk about what, Mamma?"

"Something is troubling you," her mother said. "And it
seems to be weighing more heavily on you every day."

Millie sighed. "I don't know that anyone can help me. I
miss Rhoda Jane. It's been weeks now, and she hasn't spoken to me."

"I thought that might be it," Marcia said. "God is dealing
with Rhoda Jane's heart, and it is very hard for her."

"It's a little hard on me, too," said Millie.

"What do you do when you think of Rhoda Jane?"

"Most of the time I pray for her." Millie pulled up a grass
stem and bit it. "Other times I throw rocks in the river, or
I scour our pots and pans. Pappa told me once to practice

loving my friends as God commands us in the book of Corinthians. But it's hard, Mamma. It hurts to love them when they don't love you back."

"Maybe they do," Marcia said, "and just can't show it because they are hurting, too."

They sat watching the children play for almost an hour, then Marcia noticed Fan was getting tired and hot. She bundled up Annis and the seven of them set out for home.

"What's that on the porch?" Millie asked as they came to their own house once again.

"It looks like a big box of goods," Marcia observed. "Who could have left it?"

"Back at last?" Stuart came out the door, followed by Cyril. "We thought you'd never come!"

"Pappa wouldn't let me open it," said Cyril, "not before you got back."

"It's been waiting for you for an hour," Stuart said, consulting his watch.

"Can we open it now, Pappa?" begged Fan.

"A hatchet, please!" Stuart requested. Cyril disappeared and was back in a flash with his hatchet. It took Stuart only a moment to chop the bindings and pry the lid from the crate.

"Just newspapers," said Don in dismay.

"I think there may be something underneath," said Marcia, laughing. "The newspapers are just packing. Though I think I will keep them and read them."

"What do you suppose we have in here?" asked Stuart, shoving his hand under the papers. "What would Aunt Wealthy send . . . Ahhhrghh!" He gripped his elbow with the other hand, his face twisted in pain.

"What's wrong, Pappa?" Zillah cried. "What is it?"

176

"It bit me!" Stuart said, trying to jerk his arm from the crate. Adah and Zillah backed away, eyes huge. Don grabbed his father's arm and tried to help him pull it out. Fan picked up the hatchet, but Marcia grabbed her shoulders.

"Honestly, Stuart," she said. "And we wonder where the boys come up with their pranks!"

Stuart laughed and pulled out a pattern with a note pinned to it. "It's for you, dear," he said, handing it to Marcia. "And it did bite me." He squeezed a bead of blood from his finger where the pin had pricked him. "It went in under the fingernail. Perhaps we should remove the news-papers first." He set them carefully in a pile beside the box.

"Remnants!" said Don, leaning over to get the first look. "Aunt Wealthy sent remnants!"

"Of course she did," Millie said, "and patterns, no doubt." There were patterns, catalogs, caramel candy she had made herself, small tops and yo-yos for the young children, and a set of paints for Zillah.

"Books!" yelled Don, just as they thought they had reached the bottom of the crate. "She sent books!" Stuart pulled them out one at a time to be admired. "*Tales of a Grandfather, Anna Ross*, and *Ruth Lee*, novels by James Fenimore Cooper, and finally, *Cooper's Naval History of the United States*. Ru, you will enjoy this one, I suspect. Ru?" He looked around. In fact, everyone did. "Where's Ru? I thought he was with you today?"

"No," Marcia said. "He stayed home with Cyril. Didn't you hear the story of the spilled paint?"

"Paint?" Stuart said blankly. Cyril started edging for the steps, but Stuart caught him by the collar. "What paint?"

Marcia quickly described the accident. "Where is your brother, Cyril?"

"He stayed at the river," Cyril said, "on account of he didn't want to walk home buck naked, and our clothes was all wet."

"Did you wear your wet clothes home?" Marcia asked.

"Nope," Cyril answered self-righteously. "I knowed you wouldn't approve, Mamma. You always say that damp clothes can give you a chill. So I left them on a bush and came on home."

Millie hoped that Cyril had not met any of their neighbors while he was marching home.

"You know I do not allow you children to be alone by the river," Stuart said. "Not even Ru or Millie."

"Oh, he's not alone," Cyril said. "God did provide. Helen and Lu come along just before Mamma came home, asking for Millie. I told them Millie was out but that Ru would be glad to see them. They headed down that way."

"You were wearing your trousers at that time, weren't you?" Millie asked.

"Nope," Cyril said. "But I seen 'em comin' so I wrapped up in a tablecloth off the line."

"Did they say anything about your attire?" Stuart asked.

"Nope," Cyril said again. "They just said, 'Hail Caesar! Where's Millie?' "

"I think I'll go find Ru," Stuart said. Millie went with him, across the yard and down the hill toward the river.

They had no more than left the yard when Lu came running toward them. "Oh, Mr. Keith!" she sobbed. "Rupert has drowned!"

Stuart didn't wait to hear more; he started running toward the river's edge so fast that Millie could not keep up. When she reached the water she found Helen holding Ru's shirt and weeping.

"Oh, Millie, he's been swept away!" Helen said. "We heard a splash — it must have been Ru diving in. But all we found were his clothes!"

Stuart had run halfway down the bank, and he was walking back slowly now, looking carefully at the water. Millie left Helen and Lu and ran to him.

"They heard a splash, Pappa," she said. "He can't have been in the water long."

Stuart stopped. "They heard him jump in?"

"Yes," Millie said, starting to pull off her shoes. "I'm going in, Pappa."

Stuart grabbed her arm. "Wait. Did you see something moving? Down there in the reeds by the shore?" It did appear that there was some movement. One reed bobbed up over the others then sank down again almost to water level. *Solomon Tule, Mountain Man!*

"Ru's all right, I'm sure of it," Stuart said. "Take Helen and Lu back to the house, Millie. I'll fish him out. And Millie?" She turned to look at her father. "Leave the boy's clothes."

"Oh? Ohhhhhh!" Millie said, and she went back to her friends. "Come on," she said, "I think Ru's just diving. Pappa said to go back to the house."

"Are you sure?" Helen asked. "We have been walking up and down and up and down the bank, calling for him. How could he hold his breath that long?"

"I'm sure he is just playing a trick on you," Millie said, taking Helen's hand and pulling her to her feet. "Pappa will bring him home. We received a package from Aunt Wealthy, and it was full of books and catalogs."

"Ladies' catalogs?" Helen asked hopefully. She was always on the lookout for new fashions.

"Yes," said Millie. "Would you like to see them?" Her friends followed her to the house, and she put on a kettle to heat some water for tea.

"Where's Ru?" asked Marcia.

"He'll be along with Pappa," Millie said, and she prayed that it was true. A few minutes later, Stuart and Ru came in the door. Stuart had his arm around Ru, who was shivering in his still-damp clothes.

"Would you like a cup of tea?" asked Millie, pouring him a cup.

"Th-thanks," Ru stuttered. "You know, that river is cold if you stay under long enough. I don't know how Solomon Tule the mountain man did it."

That night when Millie took her Bible out to read it, she opened to 1 Corinthians 13:4: *Love is patient, love is kind. Lord, help me be patient with Rhoda Jane.* Millie prayed her way through the verse, sentence by sentence. *Love never fails.* Millie thought of Rhoda Jane sitting alone in her house, and of baby Elsie, somewhere far away, missing her daddy. She thought of Gordon's twisted hand, and Claudina's torn heart. *Love never fails.* Her tears made splash marks on the page.

"Marcia," Stuart said at the table the next evening, "did you know that Mrs. Chetwood is seriously ill?"

"I had not heard," Marcia said, looking worried. "Is it ague?"

Stuart nodded. "It is at the Prescotts' house, too. Effie is sick." The Prescotts were a family with five little girls. Effie, the oldest, was a frail, serious girl. Millie had spoken

to her several times when they met in town or at church and found that she loved books and music.

"Let's take them some tomatoes, Mamma," Millie said. "We have plenty in our garden, and they seemed to help Zillah and Adah when they were ill."

Marcia agreed, and they packed a basket of fresh vegetables and fruit for the Chetwoods and Prescotts. Millie tucked one of the newly arrived books, *Dunallan* by Grace Kennedy, into the basket for Effie.

They called at the Chetwoods' first, and Dr. Chetwood, who received them, was grateful for the fresh fruits and vegetables. "I can't help but think the ague that sets in this time of year is related to diet," he said. "Patients who eat fresh vegetables and meat seem to recover more quickly."

Claudina was tired from attending her mother, but she graciously offered lemonade, which was declined.

"We still have to call on Effie," Marcia said. "But do let your mamma know that she is in our prayers." Mother and daughter walked together down the road, Millie carrying the basket heavy with produce.

When they arrived at the Prescotts', they found that Mrs. Prescott was out, but Effie was reclining in a large rocking chair with a comforter over her knees. And there was Damaris Drybread, too, seated in her customary upright fashion on the edge of a chair opposite Effie. Mandy Rose was sleeping in a basket at her feet.

Millie tried not to groan. When Effie saw Marcia, she tried to rise and offer her the chair, but Marcia waved her back.

"Never mind, child. I will help myself. And Damaris. It is good to see you. How is Mandy Rose doing?"

"She is the picture of health," Damaris said, "as always. Tending her does make my duties much harder, though."

"Children tend to do that," Marcia said. "And how are you today, Effie?"

"About as usual," Effie said. "Not too sick, but not too well, either."

"As I was just saying," Damaris said, flashing a look at Marcia, "if Effie would just make up her mind to be well, then she would be."

"I have tried, Miss Drybread," Effie said with tears coming to her eyes. "I want so much to be able to help my own mamma. I've tried to believe that my sickness was all imagination, as you said, but I can't. It's too real."

"You don't look terribly well," observed Marcia.

"Of course she'll wear a distressed countenance as long as she imagines she is sick," Damaris said. "And you, Marcia, are making matters worse."

Marcia didn't reply, so Millie took the book and put it in Effie's hands.

"Oh, thank you," Effie cried. "I love books!"

"A novel?" Damaris sniffed. "If you are really sick, you should read nothing but the Bible."

"The teachings of this book are so fully in agreement with those of the Scriptures that I cannot think it will hurt the child," Marcia said gently.

"I love my Bible," Effie said. "I could never do without it. Its words are sweet as honey to me. But reading other good books seems just like talking with a Christian friend. I learn so much from them."

At that moment Mrs. Prescott came in and greeted her visitors. "Marcia! How sweet of you to check on us. And Miss Drybread! It is very kind of you to come to call when you have a little one of your own to care for."

"I try to attend to every duty," Damaris explained, "and I feel I have a duty to perform here. I've been thinking a good deal about you, Effie, trying to find out why your afflictions have been sent. I've concluded that they are a punishment for your sins, and that when you repent and reform, your health will be better."

"Sins?" Mrs. Prescott asked, coming to her daughter's side.

"As I said, I have a duty to speak up. You know I never indulge in vanities of dress, and will never tolerate it in Mandy. But that has been one of your sins, Effie Prescott — bows and even flowers and feathers on your bonnets, and knots of bright ribbon at your throat and in your hair. It's sinful, and you may depend you'll be afflicted till you have given it up."

"I know I am a sinner," Effie said, tears gathering in her eyes. "But as for the flowers and bows, I don't believe you are right. You are a Job's comforter, and God reproved those men for talking so to him."

"Miss Drybread?" Millie asked sweetly, "Do you remember what Jesus said about taking the beam from your own eye before trying to remove the splinter from your brother's eye?"

"Millie!" Marcia's voice was full of reproof and it pierced to Millie's heart.

"I apologize, Miss Drybread," Millie began, but she did not get to finish.

"How dare you!" Damaris rose to her feet, scooping up Mandy Rose's basket on the way. "There is no Christian spirit about you, Millie Keith. Your mother does well to rebuke you, and she should do more. And you, Effie! You don't like faithful dealing. You don't want to be told of your

sins. Very well, Miss Prescott, I wash my hands of you. I shake off the dust of my feet against you." She stalked from the house, leaving Effie quivering from head to foot.

"Is God punishing me, Mother? Is that why I am ill so often? I love Jesus, and desire only His love. I couldn't bear it if He were angry with me!"

"Of course He is not, dearest," Mrs. Prescott said, stroking her hair. "How could the Savior who was willing to die for you be angry with one of His poor little lambs? Every one of us sins every day, but I know you ask His forgiveness. He loves you, dear one." Marcia and Millie agreed. But Marcia was watching Damaris as she walked down the road.

"Poor Damaris," she said. "How terribly lonely she must be. Perhaps you can include her in your prayers, Millie."

Can I pray for God to keep her far away from me? Millie was glad that some prayers were private. *Of every soul in Pleasant Plains, Damaris is the only one I cannot grow to like even a little.*

That evening when Millie took out her Bible, the list of family and friends fell out. Her heart tugged at her as she picked it up off the floor. *Have I been practicing loving my family and friends? I've been doing better with the boys. And I have been praying for Rhoda Jane every day. How could I love any better?*

Before she could even think about the answer, her father's words came flooding back to her: *"If you really want to see what God can do, practice on your enemies."*

Millie groaned. "Pappa could not possibly mean that I have to practice love on that horrible Damaris Drybread!" Yet even as the words came out of her mouth, Millie knew that Pappa did mean just that. And so did Jesus. *How can I call myself a Christian if I am not willing to do what I know Jesus wants me to do?*

"It's not possible!" Millie cried, arguing with herself.

But of course it was possible. God had created the stars and the moon. All He had to do to make her love Damaris Drybread was to change Millie's heart.

"I don't want my heart changed! I don't _want_ to love her!" exclaimed Millie. But she could not block the words out of her mind: _"It takes a lot of work—and courage, too."_

Millie gritted her teeth and took out her quill. _Damaris Drybread._ She wrote the name quickly at the bottom of her prayer list.

What have I done? She couldn't erase the ink. The name was at the very bottom of the page. All she had to do was tear it off, and it would be gone forever . . .

Jesus, Millie prayed, _help me want to love her._

Immediately, she tucked the paper back in her Bible.

CHAPTER

13

The Price of Freedom

*Live as free men, but do not use
your freedom as a cover-up
for evil; live as servants
of God.*

1 PETER 2:16

*K*a-BOOM! The voice of the cannon jolted Millie awake, announcing the rising of the sun.

"In-dee-pen-dence Daaaaay!" Cyril yelled in the room next door. "Waahoo! Get me a match, I'm gonna blow something up!"

"Cyril!" Stuart's voice carried down the hall from his room. "You stay in bed until I get up. And you are not to fire any crackers unless I am with you. Do you understand?"

"Yes, Pappa." There was silence, then a giggle from Don.

"And you will not connive anyone else to light them for you. You will not drop them by accident into the fire, the stove, or the furnace at the smithy."

"Aw, Pappa!"

Don and Cyril had been working odd jobs for weeks and had spent every last cent they earned on firecrackers. Every time Millie took their overalls to the washtub she found a few more when she turned the pockets inside out.

Five minutes passed.

"Pappa? Are you up yet?"

"No, son. I am sound asleep. I am dreaming that my children let me sleep late on this holiday."

"Long as you're dreaming," Cyril suggested, "how 'bout some sleep walkin'? We could go down the hill and light one or two off before breakfast."

"Not one more word," Stuart warned. There came a long, muffled groan from Cyril's room.

"Not one more sound," Stuart added.

Millie gave up on sleep, rolled out of bed, went to the kitchen, and started breakfast. Ru had been up before the

sun, milking the cow and feeding the chickens. Marcia had been up during the night with Annis, who was fussy.

"Cyril's not up yet?" Ru asked Millie. "That's surprising."

"He would be," Millie said, measuring flour into a bowl, "but Pappa is making him wait."

"That's just as well. Belle doesn't like the sound of the cannon; I don't think she will like crackers at all. And I don't want him throwing them where the hens might gobble them down before they blow up."

Millie shuddered at the vision of exploding chickens. She finished mixing her batter and poured a ladleful onto the hot griddle. The edges of the pancake sizzled as the dough spread, and bubbles appeared almost instantly and burst, leaving holes in the batter. Millie waited until the holes around the edges appeared dry, just as Celestia Ann had taught her, then she scooted the spatula under the pancake and tried to flip it. Half of it stuck to the griddle and the other half folded over it, making a sandwich of pancake with burnt crusts and oozing dough in the middle. "Griddle's too hot," said Millie.

"I think you are right," Ru agreed, opening a window to let out the smoke that had started to curl up from the cast iron.

Millie used the spatula to scoot the griddle across the cooktop to a cooler corner, and she scraped off the burnt pancake. She let the griddle cool for a moment, then dropped some butter on it and spread it quickly with the spatula as it melted.

The next pancake was perfect.

"I knew I could do it," Millie said, admiring the golden brown disk.

"I never doubted you," Ru assured her. "Can I have that one, or are you going to frame it and put it on the wall?" Ru ate the next four pancakes off the griddle, and he took the burnt one to the chickens before the rest of the family came down.

"Where's Celestia Ann?" asked Fan when she saw the pile of pancakes.

"At her own home," Ru said. "Millie made these."

The family seated themselves, and Stuart gave thanks for the meal.

Millie served her mother and father first. Stuart put a slab of butter between each of his pancakes and drizzled maple syrup over the top of the stack. The children waited as he cut the cakes with his fork. He hesitated only a fraction of a moment before he put the pancakes in his mouth and started to chew.

"Delicious!" he declared.

"Yankee-doodle-dooo!" Don crowed. "Pass the pancakes!"

Breakfast was eaten to the occasional booming of cannon in the distance.

After the meal, Stuart took the children outside to fire some crackers while Millie and Marcia prepared the little ones for an outing. The entire town was meeting in front of the courthouse that morning for a parade. A good deal of cooking had gone on the day before in the Keiths' kitchen, and a large basket was sent to the church. Everyone in town was invited to dinner there after the parade.

Marcia and Millie had their hands full for an hour or so as they dressed the children and themselves for the grand occasion. The Keiths made a good show as they walked toward the courthouse, the girls all in white muslin and blue ribbons, the boys in their neat Sunday suits, each with a flower or tiny

nosegay in his buttonhole—but Cyril and Don's pockets bulged suspiciously.

They reached the courthouse just before nine. A large platform had been erected, a wonderfully large flagstaff had been planted in front of the courthouse, and the Stars and Stripes were floating from its top. Millie turned around and found herself standing next to the Lightcaps.

"Hello, Rhoda Jane," she said quietly.

Rhoda Jane nodded.

"Hi, Millie! Look what Gordy made us!" Emmaretta and Min were waving little flags with twenty-four stars and thirteen stripes. Gordon had regained the use of the thumb and little finger of his right hand, and although he couldn't do fine carving, it didn't stop him from making toys for the little girls. The Keiths saw Gordon weekly at church, and Stuart started a comfortable conversation with him. Millie longed to be able to talk like that with Rhoda Jane again, but Rhoda Jane answered each of Millie's comments with a single syllable.

Finally Mr. Grange rose to give his speech and read the Declaration of Independence. When he read "all men are created equal, that they are endowed by their Creator with certain unalienable Rights," Ru snorted.

"You suppose the person who broke our window is listening to that?" he asked.

One speech did not seem to be enough for Mr. Grange. After he had declared freedom in the land, he started another. Mr. Grange tended to be long-winded, and when a young fellow in the back called for freedom after he had been speaking for almost an hour, there was general laughter.

Then Reverend Lord rose, and Mr. Tittlebaum with him. The minister led the old gentleman to the stairs and held his arm as he made his way up onto the platform.

"Many of you know Mr. Tittlebaum as a member of our church"—Reverend Lord's booming voice reached out over the crowd—"but most of you, I imagine, don't know his story. I asked him to tell it to us today."

Mr. Tittlebaum started to speak, but his voice was too quiet to be heard over the boisterous children and chattering crowd.

"Quiet!" Reverend Lord thundered, and the people who had been talking looked at each other sheepishly.

"My name is James Tittlebaum," the old man said, "and I want to tell you something important. I don't rightly remember how old I am this July 4." The crowd laughed, and Mr. Tittlebaum continued. "But I do remember how old I was when the United States of America was born. I was sixteen when I left my home in Connecticut and marched to join George Washington at Brooklyn, New York. I remember the call that went out for volunteers: 'Be roused and alarmed to stand forth in our just and glorious cause. Join . . . march on, this shall be your warrant: play the man for God, and for the cities of our God! May the Lord of Hosts, the God of the armies of Israel, be your leader.'"

Even the boys were listening now, leaning forward.

"I thought I was ready to fight for freedom," he laughed. "I thought wrong. I'd have run if I'd knowed what was facing us. I joined up with General Washington and eight thousand men, but there were twenty thousand British, and it was a slaughter. The British overwhelmed us. They cut off William Alexander and the Delaware militia, trapped 'em on top of a ridge, with an ocean of redcoats between them and us. I saw our militia plant their colors—a man ran it to the top of the ridge and pushed the pole hard into the ground, dodging musketballs all the way up. We tried to get to them." The old man gazed into space, and Millie was sure he was seeing a flag on a faraway hill. "Five times we tried, throwing ourselves at the British lines, good men dying each time. Five times we failed. And then they moved up the ridge like a red plague of muskets and bayonets, and we saw the colors fall."

There was a hush across the crowd. "That's when I knew what freedom was. I thought about the man I had seen plant the flag. He was dead. He had died in the dirt of that ridge, but he wasn't fighting for a hill. He was fighting for the United States of America. He was fighting for freedom." Mr. Tittlebaum wiped his hand across his mouth. "In the camp that night, and in the rain the next day, the knowledge of death was with us. We were less than seven thousand now, and low on powder and shot. General Washington had only three choices: fight to the death, surrender the Continental Army, or retreat. And the only path of retreat was across the East River, a mile wide and under British guns. That night the order came. Under cover of darkness we started the retreat, using small boats, moving as silently as possible. But there were too many men and too few boats. As dawn approached we knew the British would soon see how few of us remained and attack at once. Then a fog began to rise out of the ground and off of the river. It covered both camps, and it lingered even as the sun rose higher. George Washington himself was in the last boat to cross the river—and with that boat, the fog lifted. The British began firing, but it was too late. General Washington was out of range and the Continental Army was saved, without a single man killed during the escape!"

"I knew that day that God was with George Washington. I knew it at Valley Forge, when I lost my toe to frostbite, took a fever, and shook like I would die. The General himself stopped by my hut to take my hand and talk to me about Jesus. I could feel it on him—the favor of God. And I could see the result that day in Yorktown, when the British threw down their muskets and finally admitted what we knew all along: we were free men, with no king but God!"

A roar went up from the crowd, and Reverend Lord and Celestia Ann rose and walked onto the platform. Reverend Lord shook Mr. Tittlebaum's hand, then a line formed, every person in town filing past one by one to say thank you.

"Is that the same hand George Washington shook?" Zillah asked in awe.

"The very same," Mr. Tittlebaum replied. "Though, I confess, I've washed it once or twice since then."

Cyril offered him a silver Liberty dime to see the missing toe.

"Deal," Mr. Tittlebaum said, and he reached in his pocket and pulled out a tobacco sack. Cyril looked at the sack wide-eyed. "Let's have the dime."

Cyril fished it out of his pocket and handed it over.

"Here you go," Mr. Tittlebaum said. He opened the sack and emptied it into his hand.

"Hey!" Cyril said. "There's nothin' in it!"

"'Course not," Mr. Tittlebaum laughed. "The toe's missin'!" He dropped Cyril's dime into his pocket. "Let that be a lesson to you, youngster. Be sure of what you're paying for."

"Why the long face, son?" Stuart asked when they went back to their seats. Cyril explained, but Stuart just laughed.

"You got what you paid for," he said. "And it's a lesson well learned."

"Cheer up," said Gordon. "You aren't the first one to fall for it, and you won't be the last. Mr. Tittlebaum could buy a farm with the money he's made from that missing toe. Why don't you invite Millie over for supper, Rhoda Jane?"

"I'm afraid I have other plans," Rhoda Jane said. "Sorry."

Gordon shook his head. "Are you coming, Ma?"

"*It's* coming," Mrs. Lightcap said. "It's coming again, worse than before. I can feel it out in the swamp, waiting."

"What's coming?" asked Zillah.

"Death. It's come back again, just like the year it took my husband. I hate that swamp with every bone in my body."

"Don't worry too much," Gordon whispered to Millie. "She says that every year."

196

CHAPTER

14

Unanswered Questions

But I tell you who hear me: Love your enemies, do good to those who hate you, bless those who curse you, pray for those who mistreat you.

LUKE 6:27–28

oe Roe is dead." Ru had just come in from helping Gordon at the stable.

"What?" Marcia froze with a plate halfway to the table.

"He's dead. The shaking ague took him."

"Are you sure, Ru?" Millie asked. "We saw him at the parade and he was fine. Are you sure this isn't one of Mrs. Lightcap's . . . ideas?"

"I don't think it is," Ru said. "Gordon is making the coffin. Mrs. Lightcap said he'd better make a lot of them."

Dr. Chetwood stopped by that evening and confirmed that it was true. The shaking ague had taken Joe's life in less than a day. "The sickly season is setting in unusually early and with uncommon severity. It's what we can expect with this weather, I'm afraid. We haven't had a drop of rain now, scarcely a cloud, for three weeks, and the marshes and pools of stagnant water on every side are teeming with miasma."

"Can we guard against it?" Marcia asked, picking up Annis.

"Keep the children and yourselves out of the sun during the heat of the day, and do not, on any account, allow them to be exposed to the night air and dew. You may get off lightly, as I think the air may be healthy on this hill."

"Thank you," Stuart said. "We will do our best to follow your advice."

The ague did seem to spread from the swamp, striking one household and then another, taking giant steps toward the town itself. Dr. Chetwood's carriage could be seen at all hours of the day and heard at all hours of the night.

Millie's Courageous Days

Marcia, Mrs. Chetwood, Mrs. Prior, and Millie went door to door among their neighbors, giving aid where they could, bringing baskets of fresh food, and offering comfort and prayer. The streets of Pleasant Plains were ghostly quiet, the heat of the sun pressing everything down during the day. The air held the heat at night, hardly cooling at all.

"Store is closed due to sickness," Ru said, coming back from town one day without the lamp oil Stuart had sent him for. "There's a sign on the door. And Dr. Chetwood gave me this." He held up a yellow cloth. "Folks are putting them in their windows when they have someone sick. Effie Prescott's down again, and Minerva Lightcap, too."

"I expect we will have to wait for our lamp oil," said Marcia.

Gordon Lightcap had taken his mother's advice, and many coffins were leaning against the front of the stable. One by one they were taken away by grieving families. The congregation met more often in the graveyard than they did in the church building, saying good-bye to loved ones. Mr. Tittlebaum had seen his last Independence Day, and they laid him to rest beside Joe Roe.

"Damaris was not at the funeral," Marcia said the next day as they delivered food baskets. "Have we ever stopped at her house?"

"No, Mamma," Millie said, "but she hasn't put a yellow rag in the window."

"I think we should stop today."

Millie grimaced, but when they approached the Drybread house she could see that something was wrong. The shutters were drawn in the middle of the day. And then Millie saw the yellow rag nailed to the door.

Marcia knocked on the door and it swung inward at her touch.

"Damaris?" Marcia called. "Are you home?" There was a sob from the darkness inside. Marcia pushed open the door.

Damaris was sitting in a rocking chair in the corner of the upstairs room. She held a Bible open in her lap. The small form in her arms was very, very still. Marcia went to her quickly and touched Mandy Rose's face. "Oh, Damaris," she whispered. "Mandy Rose is gone."

"Dr. Chetwood never came," Damaris said, as Marcia took Mandy Rose gently from Damaris's arms and laid her in the crib. "The Lord gives, and the Lord takes away," Damaris said. "Blessed be the name of the Lord."

"Damaris, I am so sorry."

"It's nothing to me. She wasn't my child," the woman said, standing and smoothing her skirts.

"Surely, your sister's child . . ."

"I never had a sister," Damaris said, waving at her writing table. And then she said more softly, "I never had a sister. I have been writing to solicitors, to newspapers. No one has heard of a family called Rose. I don't know . . . who she was."

"But why didn't you tell us that when Mr. Rose left the baby at our house?" Marcia asked.

"The Bible is very clear about the care of widows and orphans," Damaris said, smoothing her skirt again. "I felt it was my Christian duty to see that she was clothed and fed. I tried to find out who she really belonged to. I have sent countless letters." Her eyes, which had been avoiding the crib the whole time, suddenly came to rest on it. "Dr. Chetwood never came," she said. "All I could do was pray for her, and read the Bible. He never came."

Suddenly her thin frame shook with sobs and she sank to her knees. Marcia knelt and took her in her arms.

"What did I do wrong? I don't know what my sin was! If someone had told me, I would have repented. I would have given my very life for her!"

"You did nothing wrong, Damaris," Marcia said, rocking her. "You did something right. You loved her."

"I wish I were dead," Damaris said. "Why couldn't I have died instead of Mandy? I keep telling myself, the Lord gives and the Lord takes away. Blessed be . . ." She burst out in great sobs that seemed to come from the very depths of her soul and shook her whole body. Marcia sat on the floor, holding her. "You cry," Marcia said. "Go ahead and cry. He knows your heart is hurting, Damaris. His heart is breaking for you."

"I didn't . . . know . . . who . . . she was!" Damaris sobbed.

"I know who she was," Marcia said, rocking her. "She was your child."

Millie told herself that it was the sickness that kept people away from the churchyard when Mandy Rose was buried. The Keiths stood silently, Stuart holding the twins' hands. Marcia stood on one side of Damaris and Celestia Ann on the other as the small coffin was lowered into the ground. Millie couldn't keep her eyes from Damaris's face. It reminded her of something, someone . . . but she couldn't remember who. Stuart and Ru used shovels to fill the grave, and Zillah and Adah placed flowers they had picked on top of the freshly mounded earth. Reverend Lord read a prayer, then Damaris just turned and walked away.

"Lord, help her," Marcia prayed.

"Mamma," Fan asked as they walked home, "why did baby Mandy Rose die?"

"I don't know," Marcia said seriously.

"Is she afraid to be dead?"

"I don't think so," Marcia said. "I think she belonged to Jesus."

"I'm afraid of being dead," Don said. "I'm afraid of being put in the ground. Aren't you afraid of being dead, Mamma?"

"No," Marcia said. "Do you remember when you asked Jesus to be your Savior?"

Don nodded. "Last year I prayed with Pappa."

Stuart smiled at him.

Marcia nodded. "The Bible tells us that if Jesus is our Savior we don't have to be afraid of death. It says, 'Since the children have flesh and blood, he too shared in their humanity so that by his death he might destroy him who holds the power of death—that is the devil—and free those who all their lives were held in slavery by their fear of death.' That means that Jesus came to earth and had a body that died. He rose again to show us that we don't have to be afraid when our bodies die. We are going to be with Him."

"Was the man who brought baby Mandy Rose to Miss Drybread a fat angel?" Fan asked.

"Why would you think that?" Stuart asked, surprised.

"I heard him singing when he left," Fan said. "The same song I heard when I jumped down from the door into heaven."

Marcia and Stuart looked at each other. "Some people have entertained angels unawares," Stuart said.

"I didn't hear anything," said Cyril. "And why would an angel give a baby to Miss Drybread, anyways? Pappa, did Jesus give Mr. Tittlebaum back his toe when he got to heaven?"

"I expect He did," said Stuart.

"Well, where'd He keep it all this time? I mean before Mr. Tittlebaum got there?"

"I don't know, son," his father replied. "There are a great many things that I don't know about heaven. I'm going to have to wait to find out."

Millie's mind kept going back to Damaris's face. Suddenly she knew where she had seen that look before, hopeless and lost—on Mandy Rose, the day she was left at the Keiths'! A picture of the baby's thin, pinched face flashed through her mind, and Millie almost gasped. *Is that the way You see Damaris, Lord? Someone lost and alone who just needs to be cleaned up and loved? Forgive me for the way I have treated her, Lord.* Even if the fat farmer had not been an angel, God had still sent Mandy Rose to Damaris. He had trusted her to take care of His precious little one until He called her home. *That's what Mamma sees in Damaris! That's what Jesus sees in her.*

At home again, Millie shut the door to her room and took out her writing pad. *Love never fails. Give me the courage to love as You would, Jesus.* She prayed silently, spilling her heart to Jesus, and then began to write:

Dear Damaris,

I have not treated you with respect, and I am ashamed of my behavior. I want you to know that I believe God sent Mandy Rose to you because He needed someone to love her. I know you were His very first choice. I hope that someday I can do as good a job of loving and caring for my own child as you did with Mandy.

You said that you have never had a sister. If you will have me, I will be proud to be your sister in Christ.

1 Corinthians 13:4,
Millie Keith

Unanswered Questions

Millie folded the letter and sealed it with wax. The next day when she carried food baskets with her mother, Millie put it in her pocket. They had dropped off the last basket when they stopped by Damaris's house. The shutters were still closed.

Marcia knocked and called, but there was no answer.

"Perhaps she needs the time alone," Marcia said. "I don't feel we should barge in on her."

Millie took the letter out of her pocket and slipped it under the door.

CHAPTER 15

An Impossible Thing

Hope deferred makes the heart sick, but a longing fulfilled is a tree of life.

PROVERBS 13:12

An Impossible Thing

*T*he sun seemed determined to draw every drop of moisture from the ground of Pleasant Plains, to wilt every plant, and to blister the new paint on houses and barns. Stuart gave up going to the office, as there was no business in town.

He spent his days watching over the little children down by the river while Millie and Marcia took care of the cooking and preparing food for the neighbors. Millie envied the younger children their freedom when she carried a picnic down the steps and found them all submerged to the eyeballs, like so many hippos among the reeds, but she wouldn't have given up helping her mother for the world. Millie followed in her footsteps as she visited the sick neighbors, bringing food, comfort, and help. Stuart and Ru watched over the Keith household, making sure the children were inside before sundown every day to keep them from the night air. Stuart wouldn't let them set foot outside until well after the dew was gone.

"The air on this hill must be healthy," Dr. Chetwood said when he stopped by one day. "You are the only house in town with no one sick. My own family is suffering. Both Claudina and Will are down, and my wife has her hands full nursing them."

"I didn't know," Marcia said. "I will be over to help in the morning."

Dr. Chetwood nodded his thanks. "Once this fever sets in, it can take weeks to clear up. The healthy are exhausted from nursing the sick—and then they get it, too. Reverend and Mrs. Lord and that fool cow of theirs are making the rounds, cooking, cleaning, and praying, and giving people lots of milk. Well, maybe it will help. Something must. If we continue at this rate, Pleasant Plains will die."

Marcia looked at Stuart and shook her head. "Surely it's not that bad . . ."

Dr. Chetwood just sighed. "In all my years of doctoring I have never seen a season like this. I have never lost so many patients to ague. And it will continue, I'm afraid, until the rains wash it away."

"You must protect your health, doctor," Stuart said. "The whole town is depending on you, and the countryside, too."

"Well, I'm not going to do them much good until the next stagecoach arrives. I'm almost out of quinine."

"Mrs. Prior says that water from boiled willow bark can help the fever," Millie said. "She's serving willow tea to her lodgers who are ill."

"An old Indian remedy," Dr. Chetwood said. "I have heard of it, but I put no faith in it."

The next morning Millie and her mother were surprised to find Gordon Lightcap up to his elbows in suds in the Chetwoods' kitchen.

"I am impressed, Gordon," Marcia said. "I didn't know you could do laundry!"

"I heard Claudina needed help," he said, scrubbing the linen against the washboard. "So I came."

Marcia excused herself to go with Mrs. Chetwood and speak to the patients, but Millie lingered in the kitchen.

"Have you seen Claudina?" Millie asked.

"No." Gordon pulled the sheet out of the washtub and twisted it expertly to wring the excess water from it. "I don't expect to. But I can do some of her mother's work, and her mother can sit with her." He pulled his mangled hand out of the soapy water. "There are still lots of things

I can do with this hand, Millie. Lots of useful things. Like helping Mrs. Chetwood." Millie could only nod.

"Gordon, Claudina . . ."

"Doesn't love me?"

"I wasn't going to say that. It's just that her heart . . ."

"It's all right." He plunged another sheet into the tub. "I know."

Millie spent the day helping Gordon with the laundry and cooking meals to leave for the Chetwoods. She was exhausted when they finally started home.

The sun was still up, and Stuart was sitting on the porch in the shade where the hilltop breeze could cool him and Annis who sat in his lap.

Annis moaned as they reached the porch. "She's burning up, Marcia," Stuart said.

"My poor darling." Marcia leaned over and kissed Annis. "It's the fever," she sighed.

Millie's eyes filled with tears. She couldn't help but think of Mandy Rose's little grave with the wilted flowers on it.

"Mamma . . ." She couldn't keep the fear from her voice. "If we should lose her . . ."

"We will do all we can to make her well," Marcia said calmly. "Call the children in, Millie. The sun is about to set."

The family gathered in the sitting room to pray over Annis in her cradle. She was too hot and uncomfortable to allow anyone to hold her. Marcia smoothed her curls while Stuart prayed.

"Poor baby Annis," Fan said, crawling up onto Millie's lap and laying her head on Millie's shoulder. Millie wrapped her arms around her little sister. It was like hugging one of Celestia Ann's heated bricks.

"Mamma," Millie said, her throat tightening, "I think Fan may have fever, too."

Marcia touched Fan's forehead with her lips, then nodded. "I believe we need to send for the doctor, Stuart." Fan was tossing and turning on her bed by the time Dr. Chetwood arrived.

"This is the last of it," Dr. Chetwood said, setting a bottle of quinine on the table. "We won't have any more until the stagecoach arrives next week. Try to make it last and make sure they drink plenty of water. It seems to help with the fever. You know ague can run its course in a few days, or it can take two or three weeks. Even after the patient is past the crisis, recovery can be slow." He touched Annis's cheek. "Good luck, Marcia. You have helped so many other families, I had hoped you would be spared this. Stuart, I . . ." he glanced at Stuart, then took a step toward him. "Are you feeling ill, man?"

"I'm afraid I am," Stuart said weakly. "I didn't think it would come on this suddenly."

"You must go to bed right away," Dr. Chetwood ordered. "Exerting yourself at this stage could make the symptoms much more severe."

Stuart allowed himself to be put to bed, but he refused to take any quinine. "Keep it for the children, dear," he said. "I'll have a bit if I still need it when the stagecoach arrives."

"I'm sure you will be up and around by then," Marcia said.

Dr. Chetwood left, and Marcia made her patients as comfortable as she could. Millie prepared a light meal of tea and biscuits, but no one really felt like eating.

Marcia led the family in prayers, praying with special tenderness over each sick one. She pulled her rocking chair

into the hall where she could be within calling distance of each member of her family and set her Bible on her lap. Millie could see that it was open to Psalm 91, the psalm Reverend Lord had prayed over Fan so many months ago.

"I'll stay up with you, Mamma," Millie said.

"No, dear," said Marcia, looking up from her Bible. "I will need you fresh and rested in the morning."

Lord, send Your rain. Send rain to wash the fever away! Millie prayed long and hard until she fell asleep, but she awakened the next morning to find the sun already high. She threw off her covers and went to the window. The sky was hot and brassy, showing no hint of rain or relief from the heat. *Everyone in town has been praying for rain for so long. Isn't God listening?*

She met her mother carrying a pitcher of cold water up the stairs for her patients.

"Good morning," Marcia said. She looked weary. "Zillah is down this morning, but the boys are in the kitchen waiting for breakfast."

"I'll get it, Mamma, don't worry." Millie hurried to the kitchen.

Cyril and Don were sitting at the table looking forlorn.

"Pappa and Mamma need our help this morning," Millie said. "I want you to help brother Ru feed the chickens and draw water for the animals. Then you can fill the kindling box. I will have your breakfast ready when you are done." For once Cyril didn't grumble. He simply followed Don out the door to find Ru, who was already at work.

There was no change in the patients all that day, although Dr. Chetwood made his rounds and examined each one. By midday the house was an oven, with scarcely a breath of air stirring, even though every window and door had been left wide open.

Millie's Courageous Days

Marcia just closed her eyes and sighed when Cyril and Don both complained of headaches after dinner. She tucked two more patients into bed and kissed their fevered brows.

"Four of us left," she said. "Ru, I need you to go to town. I need Mrs. Prior or Mrs. Chetwood, or possibly the Lords. The quinine is gone. Pappa can't sit up. We will be needing help."

Ru nodded and left. Millie took his place, carrying bucket after bucket of water from the spring to the house for the sufferers.

Ru returned just before sunset, stopping Millie in the yard and taking the bucket of water from her hand. "No one can help us," he said. "No one can come. They all have sick ones of their own to mind—and I couldn't find the Lords. What am I going to tell Mamma, Millie? She's all done in from nursing the sick ones."

Marcia must have read the news on his face when he came in the door. "God is still with us," she said, "and He is still in control. Let's move all the children to the sitting room. It will be easier to care for them there. I'll take care of Pappa myself."

Why not move Pappa, too? Millie thought, suddenly chilled. *Is he too ill? Or even* ... she couldn't complete the thought, it was too terrible. And she didn't dare ask in front of the children. She helped move the small patients one by one onto cots and mats in the sitting room. She sighed with relief when Marcia carried a pitcher of water up to Stuart's room. *He's alive. Mamma wouldn't carry water up if he weren't.*

"Millie, will you bathe Cyril's face with a cool cloth, while I bathe Don's? And Adah, bring your Bible. You can read to us."

214

Adah brought her Bible from her room. "Which part, Mamma?"

"I've always loved Psalm 100," Marcia said. "I would like to hear it now."

" 'Shout for joy to the Lord, all the earth',," Adah began. " 'Worship the Lord with gladness; come before him with joyful songs. Know that the Lord is God. It is he who made us, and we are his; we are his people, the sheep of his pasture.' "

Cyril tossed and turned beneath the cool cloth as Adah's voice went on. Marcia joined in the last verse. " 'For the Lord is good and his love endures forever; his faithfulness continues through all generations.' "

"Water, water, water!" Cyril cried. "Please Ru, get me some cool water!"

Ru picked up the bucket and started for the door.

"Rupert!" Marcia cried. "The night air!"

"I don't think it matters, Mamma," said Ru. "Not anymore." He was back in a few moments with cool water for all the sick ones.

Marcia stood to take it from him, took two steps, and collapsed. Adah screamed. "Mamma's dying!" She fell on her knees beside her.

"Hush," Millie said, though fear shot through her. She knelt beside her sister. Marcia's face and hands were hot, but her breathing was regular. Millie loosened her clothing, ignoring the cries of the sick children. "Get a pillow for her, Ru. We won't be able to lift her." Millie made her mother as comfortable as she could on the floor, then she climbed the stairs to her father's room.

"Pappa?" she said into the darkness. "Pappa? Mamma needs you. We need you." He mumbled and tossed on the bed. His eyes were bright with fever and his cheeks

flushed red. *Delirious. He's delirious—just like Mr. Lightcap was before he died. That's what Mamma didn't want me to know.* Millie forced him to drink a cup of water, then went back downstairs.

"What are we going to do, Millie?" Ru looked helplessly around the room.

"Millie, is Mamma gonna die? Won't Aunt Wealthy come back and help us now?" Zillah cried.

"No, dear," Millie said. "Aunt Wealthy is too far away."

"Millie?" Don said quietly. "It's okay. I'm not afraid of going under the dirt anymore."

Millie caught the sob before it could escape her throat and covered her face with her hands. *We could all be in our graves before Aunt Wealthy even hears we are sick. What do I do? Lord, show me what to do! Why haven't You sent rain? We're desperate! Why are You allowing this to happen? Didn't You hear Mamma's prayers? Any of our prayers?*

Millie could almost hear Aunt Wealthy's voice. *"God calls us to a wild adventure, not a tea party, my dear. God has not answered our prayers yet with a yes or a no. And until He does, Millie, we just keep praying."*

"What are we going to do?" Ru repeated.

"First, we are going to pray," Millie said, getting down on her knees.

"We've been praying!" exclaimed Adah. "It isn't working."

"It is," Millie said firmly. "Just like it worked when we prayed for Fan. We just haven't seen the answer yet."

"Are you sure?" asked Ru. Millie didn't feel sure at all, but again, Aunt Wealthy's words came to her mind: *"Sometimes the way we feel has nothing to do with what is true."* "I'm sure," Millie replied.

Adah and Ru knelt beside her and took her hands.

"Lord," Millie prayed, "we need You. You said in Your Word we could call upon You in the day of trouble and that You would help us. We need Your help, desperately! Give us courage and keep us strong, and show us how to help our family. Please make them well, Jesus. You've *got* to heal them," pleaded Millie.

"And send help," Ru added. "Send help."

"Yes, Lord, send help quickly. Amen."

"Now what, Millie?" asked Ru.

"Now we do our best," she said. "Bring me some willow branches, Ru."

Millie put the kettle on to boil, and she peeled the willow bark into it. She boiled it and let it steep. The willow water was bitter, so she added a spoonful of honey to each cup as she fed it to her patients.

Millie forced Ru and Adah to lie down for a few hours while she tended the patients alone. Pappa had tossed and turned in the night, but he was drinking water and tea. There had been no change in the others through the long dark hours. She was exhausted when the sun came up.

"I think your tree tea is working," Ru said as he dipped up another cup. "Fan is better. Her fever's broken. Annis's too."

Millie went to Fan's cot and felt her head. It was cool and Fan was sleeping easily.

"Get me some more willow bark, Ru," Millie said. As soon as Ru was gone, Millie poured a cup of tea for her pappa and headed for the stairs. She was so exhausted that she couldn't see straight. The room swam before her eyes. *It is exhaustion, isn't it Lord? I can't get sick.* The room tilted, and then the cup was on the floor, broken to pieces. Millie was not sure how it had gotten there.

"I need someone to clean that up, God," she said. "I . . . need . . . some help. Send somebody." She felt the room tilt again and knew she was falling, but strangely, she never seemed to hit the ground. Someone's arms were around her and they half led, half carried her to the couch.

"The answer is yes," the arms said.

Millie opened her eyes. "Hello, Damaris. I don't remember the question."

"The question was, whether or not I wanted a sister in Christ. I'm not going to be good at it, I'm sure, but . . . the answer is yes. I've come to help."

"My head hurts," Millie said.

<hr />

"Hello, Millie," said Rhoda Jane.

"Uggggg." Millie didn't even try to sit up. "You would think a person could be sick in peace and quiet around here. There's been a constant racket all night."

"Really?" Rhoda Jane asked, closing the book in her lap. "Which night? You have been out of your head for a week."

"A week!" Millie tried to sit up, but pain blazed through her head. "Ow. Rhoda Jane, are the boys . . . is Don . . ."

"They are fine. Up and walking, back on their feet, as Dr. Chetwood would say. All the Keiths are on their way to recovery. You were the only one giving us the least bit of worry."

Millie tried to focus her eyes, but they wouldn't quite work. "What are you reading?" she asked.

"Oh, this? It's just a book a friend gave me a long time ago. Would you like me to read aloud?"

"Please," Millie said, closing her throbbing eyes.

"For God so loved the world that he gave his one and only Son, that whoever believes in him shall not perish but have eternal life . . ."

That's odd, Millie thought. *I think I have read that before . . . Oh, here comes Mr. Rose in his wagon. Let me just crawl up into that wagon bed and pull the buffalo robe over my head . . . We're going where, Mr. Rose? Yes, I'll find out when I get there.*

The next time she woke, Millie saw her mother sitting by her bed. "Thank goodness you are through the crisis," Marcia said. "I thought we had lost you, daughter."

"I didn't feel lost, Mamma," Millie said weakly. "It was just a long, long ride. Was Rhoda Jane here?"

"Rhoda Jane, and Gordon, and Helen and Lu, Reverend Lord and Celestia Ann . . . and Damaris Drybread. I don't know what would have become of us if she hadn't come when she did."

<hr />

Millie's recovery was much slower than that of the other Keiths. She had very little energy, and her parents would not allow her to do the least bit of housework until she was recovered. Cyril was forced to wear an apron and do dishes, much to his dismay. "It's good for his heart," Stuart said. "And his fingernails have never been cleaner."

One afternoon Millie wandered out to her swing and sat down, too tired to walk back across the yard.

"Well, look who is out of doors!" Rhoda Jane was walking across the yard toward her. "I have been waiting to talk with you, Millie Keith!"

"I have been waiting to talk with you, too," Millie said. "Were you in my room, reading the Bible?"

"Yes," Rhoda Jane said seriously. "That's why I have been waiting for you. I wanted you to hear it first, even before Gordon." Rhoda Jane sat down in the grass and pulled up her knees. "Will you forgive me for shunning you?"

"Of course I will . . ." Millie began, but Rhoda Jane interrupted. "I want to explain. When Gordon became a Christian, I was so angry with you. You were meddling with my family. I thought you had no right. But do you remember when Celestia Ann dared me to ask God for one impossible thing?"

"I don't remember that it was a dare, exactly," Millie said.

Rhoda Jane shrugged. "Well, I asked Him for the most impossible thing I could think of. I asked Him to send Damaris Drybread to my house to say she was sorry for the things she had said and done when my father was dying. It was about five days after Mandy Rose's funeral. Emmaretta was sick, burning with the fever, and Ma was in no shape to help her. I had been watching over her all day when someone knocked at the door. Gordon answered it. I wouldn't have let her in." Rhoda Jane paused a moment, then went on. "Damaris clutched her Bible to her chest. She walked right in, stood in the exact spot she had three years ago . . . and she said she was sorry. She opened her Bible and read to me, all about love. I found the verses later, after she had gone. "Love is patient, love is kind. It does not envy, it does not boast, it is not proud. . . ." It went on and on and I knew that it was true. The only thing I could think of as she was reading was that I know people who act like that—the Keiths. And now I know why they act like that. Because God is real, and they belong to Him. And I decided I wanted to belong to Him, too — more than anything else on earth. Only I was afraid He wouldn't want me."

"Of course He would!" exclaimed Millie.

"I know. I read the New Testament," Rhoda Jane continued. "Jesus died for me. I want to ask Him to take away my sins, and to be my King. But I waited for you, Millie, because I want you to pray with me."

There were tears in Millie's eyes as they began the prayer of salvation, and tears in Rhoda Jane's before they finished.

"Someone very wise once told me that life with God is an adventure," Millie said, "greater and wilder than I could ever imagine. She was right."

"I hope there's room in your adventure for a friend," said Rhoda Jane, sitting on the swing beside Millie. "Because I am coming, too. How high can this thing go?"

Are Millie's trials finally over?
Has the epidemic passed?
What will happen to little Elsie Dinsmore?

Find out in:

MILLIE'S REMARKABLE JOURNEY

Book Three
of the
*A Life of Faith:
Millie Keith* Series

Available at your local bookstore

Collect our other
A Life of Faith Products!

A Life of Faith: Elsie Dinsmore Series

Check out
www.alifeoffaith.com

 Get news about Millie and her cousin Elsie

 Find out more about the 19th Century world they live in

Learn to live a life of faith like they do

 Learn how they overcome the difficulties we all face in life

Find out about Millie and Elsie products

Join our girls' club

A Life of Faith Books
"It's Like Having a Best Friend From Another Time"